A
VERY
BOOKISH
MURDER

BOOKS BY DEE MACDONALD

Ally McKinley Mystery Series
Murder in the Scottish Highlands
Murder at the Loch

Kate Palmer Mystery Series
A Body in the Village Hall
A Body in Seaview Grange
A Body at the Tea Rooms
A Body at the Altar
A Body on the Beach
A Body at Lavender Cottage
A Body in a Cornish Village

The Runaway Wife
The Getaway Girls
The Silver Ladies of Penny Lane
The Golden Oldies Guesthouse
The Sunshine Club

A VERY BOOKISH MURDER

DEE MACDONALD

Bookouture

Published by Bookouture in 2025

An imprint of Storyfire Ltd.
Carmelite House
50 Victoria Embankment
London EC4Y 0DZ

www.bookouture.com

The authorised representative in the EEA is Hachette Ireland
8 Castlecourt Centre
Dublin 15 D15 XTP3
Ireland
(email: info@hbgi.ie)

ISBN: 978-1-83618-252-8
eBook ISBN: 978-1-83618-251-1

ONE

Snow might still have been lingering on the mountaintops in the Western Highlands of Scotland, but further down the valley in the sleepy village of Locharran, the earth had sprung to life once more, with wildflowers blooming in the warm sunshine, and, best of all as far as Ally McKinley was concerned, *guests*! The great British public were on the move again after the soggy, unsettled Easter weather, and Ally had reopened The Auld Malthouse B&B, where she hoped to welcome visitors into her newly spring-cleaned, polished premises, with its three en-suite double bedrooms.

Her last guests had been back in November when she had welcomed some hardy hillwalkers into the old malthouse, but from now until October was the time when she must make her money. And prove to her doubting offspring that this was truly a great venture. As well as it being a wonderful *adventure*. Jamie and Carol, her adult children, had ridiculed her idea of escaping the rat race at her late age, a retired widow, then sixty-six. It was a crazy idea, they said, not least because she'd fallen in love with such an old building but had also spent all of her money converting it. What was *that* all about at *her* time of life? And why would you want to leave Edinburgh? they asked. And your cosy little flat?

Ally had been on a holiday, recently retired from her hectic life as a television researcher in Edinburgh, when she first saw and fell in love with the old building in its magical setting on the heather-covered hillside in the shadow of the magnificent turreted Locharran Castle, home of the earls of Locharran. The current earl, Hamish Sinclair, owned most of the surrounding area, including the village, the moorlands and several lochs.

Yes, it was for sale, everyone said, but there was no 'For Sale' board up to advertise the fact, and so she'd had to do her first bit of sleuthing to find out who owned it. That took time, as did the conversion, and it also took a great deal of money.

A couple of years later, her sleuthing and investment had paid off and she was really beginning to feel settled in her new home. There was her relationship with Ross Patterson, the handsome (supposedly) retired vet, who'd just happened to be on duty when she took her Labrador puppy, Flora, in for her jabs. What a lovely man he was, and what a wonderful, and very unexpected, relationship they had at their late ages! There was her friendship with Linda, who lived in the village; her friendship with Magda, the earl's wife; and, not least, her friendship with the earl himself, Hamish Sinclair.

Ally and her old malthouse had done well last year, and she was determined to build on that and make it the best little B&B in the Highlands. And so, when another of her neighbours, the rather eccentric artist Desdemona Morton, called in to ask if she could accommodate a group of ladies on a writers' retreat at the beginning of May, Ally was delighted.

'How many ladies?' Ally asked.

'Five,' Desdemona confirmed. 'They're from the Literary Ladies Writing Retreat group. It's organised by an old friend of mine, Penelope Fortescue-Rawlins. They go somewhere different every year. Last year it was Greece; this year it's

Locharran. They have lectures, writing exercises, et cetera, with the ultimate aim of becoming published authors. You know the sort of thing?'

'Not really,' Ally admitted.

'It's an excuse to join up with other like-minded women and have a holiday at the same time. Every year they invite a published author to join them to lead the workshops and share their wisdom, and the star of the show this year is Jodi Jones.'

'I know Jodi Jones's books! I've read several,' Ally exclaimed. 'And I love them – they're *very* racy.' She paused. 'I have one double and two twin-bedded rooms. Will that do, do you think?'

Desdemona nodded. 'Jodi'll need a room to herself, of course, and the other four will share the other two rooms.'

'Where do you come into all of this?' Ally asked, looking at Desdemona quizzically.

'Jodi and I knew each other at university, along with Penelope,' Desdemona replied. 'Jodi went on to study literature and became a successful writer, while I concentrated on my art. Penelope read history, but it was always horses and rich, aristocratic men that really interested her! But we've all stayed in touch. There are thirteen in the group altogether, and the others will be staying at the Craigmonie Hotel, where the writing retreat will be taking place, but they didn't have enough rooms for them all.'

'Thirteen?' Ally raised an eyebrow. 'I hope that's not going to be an unlucky number!'

'Nonsense!' said Desdemona. 'Of course not.'

The ladies had duly arrived on the Sunday evening.

Jodi Jones, the well-known writer, was a tall, attractive woman in her sixties, with a long scarf draped artfully around her neck. The leader of the group, Penelope Fortescue-Rawlins, was a hearty woman with a very loud voice and a very upper-crust accent. Then there was Joyce Williams, also tall, white-haired and intense; along with Millie Day, fiftyish, small and mousy in appearance; plus Brigitte Atkins, who was French, married to an Englishman and, in her forties, considerably younger than the others.

Prompted by Jodi and encouraged by the others, it was this little group that invited Ally, on their first evening together, to join them at the Craigmonie Hotel the following afternoon to see what their group was all about and to listen to Jodi's first talk.

And so, at precisely five minutes to three that following afternoon, Ally found herself amidst thirteen women of various shapes and sizes, only five of whom she knew slightly. Callum Dalrymple, the manager of the Craigmonie, had allocated them the Garden Room, which was a comfortable size for a dozen or so people and had a wall of glass doors looking out onto the garden, towards the river. She'd picked up a leaflet which listed all the ladies, where they came from and what they wrote.

Her own five had proved to be ideal guests so far, all having settled for continental breakfast and leaving tidy rooms, much to the relief of Morag McConnachie, Ally's cleaner. Morag lived in the village with her husband, Murdo, who was the post-man, and between them, they knew all the gossip and goings-on in Locharran.

Before Ally had time to study the list in detail, Jodi arrived with clipboard and notes, calling out, 'As Ally McKinley is our honoured guest, she must sit in the front row.' There followed some applause, although eight of these women hadn't the faintest idea who she was.

Ally, having hoped to remain inconspicuous at the back, was now persuaded to move forward and found herself next to a slim, pretty woman with red hair and an Irish accent.

'You're goin' to enjoy this,' the woman prophesied.

Jodi was attired in a blue linen maxi dress, with a very beautiful long, blue-and-green silk scarf around her neck. What was it about this woman and her scarves? Ally wondered. It must obviously be her signature look, she decided.

'We'd also particularly like to welcome Della Moran,' Jodi continued, 'who is new to our group and has come all the way from Northern Ireland.' She indicated the red-haired woman next to Ally. More applause.

Everyone had pens, notebooks and eager expressions. Ally had never thought about writing and wondered if this experience might possibly convert her.

'God, I'd kill for that scarf!' murmured Della Moran.

'Me too!' agreed Ally. 'It's really beautiful.' She looked sideways at Della. 'And it would look great on you with your red hair.'

Ally had had auburn locks herself at one time, but the approaching grey now necessitated some expensive highlights and lowlights. Nevertheless, a fabulous scarf like that would make a very eye-catching addition to her wardrobe.

Jodi cleared her throat, waved her pen in the air and began to talk. She spoke eloquently about writing in general, about her online critiques for aspiring writers, and about publishing and publishers, that ultimate aim. All went well for about forty minutes until Jodi began to speak about original ideas. 'It's so important you come up with some new ideas, something original that no one else has thought of.'

Suddenly Della, the red-haired Irish lady, stood up and shouted, 'That's all very well, Jodi Jones, but I am here to accuse you of downright plagiarism! Your latest novel, *Love Bites*, is almost a replica of my book, *Crossed Swords*, which was published four years ago!'

For a moment, there was a horrified silence, then mayhem ensued.

'Nonsense!' some of the women called out.

'Jealousy!' shouted some others.

'No,' said Della firmly, 'if you bothered to read these books, you'd see exactly what I mean.'

'Don't be so bloody ridiculous,' Jodi said. 'You're grasping at straws, Della Moran. Just because my book sold and yours did *not!*'

Everyone was on their feet now, the class in chaos, but no one was able to stop Della Moran, who was still in full flow. 'Everyone who read my book has commented on how you copied my story! *Everyone!*'

'We haven't come all this way to hear you two arguing,' Penelope shouted in her clipped, authoritative tone, coming round to stand between Della and Jodi.

Jodi, breathing heavily, called out, 'Let's take a coffee break, everyone. Miss Moran here has, for reasons of her own, disrupted this class with her ridiculous claims. We all need to calm down and' – here she consulted her watch – 'I suggest we reconvene in twenty minutes at four o'clock.' With a look of pure hatred at Della, she turned and marched out of the room.

Now everyone was on their feet, voices raised, questioning, horrified. All attention was focussed on Della Moran, who, far from being in any way repentant, was standing in front of the group where Jodi had just been.

'She copied my bloody plot, and the only reason I'm here today is to expose her for what she is. And how many other authors' plots has she stolen? I'm here to tell you that *this is what she does!*'

There were gasps all round. Of belief or disbelief? Ally wondered.

'No, no, she writes great books!' someone said.

'I *love* her books!' said someone else.

At this point, two waiters came hurriedly in, looking a little bemused, with pots of tea, coffee and biscuits. There was a rush towards both the refreshments and the ladies' room, everyone chatting animatedly and excitedly.

It was one of her guests, Joyce Williams, who nudged Ally. 'I bet you didn't expect things to be this lively,' she said.

Ally certainly hadn't but, not having read Della's book, was in no position to comment.

Slowly, everyone began to gravitate back towards their seats, balancing cups and saucers, waiting expectantly for Jodi's return and, hopefully, some more exciting revelations. But after fifteen minutes there was still no sign of Jodi. Ally reckoned she'd probably gone through to the bar for a stiff drink, and who could blame her?

They waited and they waited. Della was still surrounded by some excited women and appeared to be in her element. 'This is the woman who's charging you a fortune to come up here, mainly to flog her own bloody books and which are full of other people's ideas because she hasn't got any of her own!' Della said, loudly and clearly.

Ally decided this might be a good time to make her escape. She could make the excuse that she was checking on Jodi's whereabouts, and then slip quietly away.

'I'm going to check on Jodi,' she called out to Joyce, who was standing nearby with Penelope and Millie next to the biscuits. 'I have to say that this has been more interesting than I could ever have imagined!'

They giggled. 'I bet she's having a drink in the bar,' Joyce said, echoing Ally's thoughts. 'I'll come with you.'

Ally first glanced into the bar to see if Jodi had opted to go there, but there was no sign of her. She then pushed the door of the ladies' room open, followed by Joyce, but the place appeared to be empty. There were four cubicles, but one was closed with an 'Out of Order' sign hanging on the door.

'She's hardly likely to be in there!' Joyce said.

Nevertheless, Ally gave the door a push because it didn't

appear to be locked and, just at first, it wouldn't open. There seemed to be some obstacle behind it. When, with much effort, she, together with Joyce, succeeded in pushing the door half open, they saw the cause of this impediment.

There, in a heap on the floor, with that beautiful scarf bound tightly round her neck, was Jodi Jones.

TWO

Joyce screamed. Ally, too horrified to make a sound, kneeled by Jodi, whose face was red and flushed with small patches of broken blood vessels marring the surface of her skin. And on the underside of her chin were livid scratch marks where she'd obviously tried to fight against the force of the scarf biting into her neck. With shaking hands, Ally loosened the scarf and pulled it as gently as she could from around Jodi's neck. She knew that she shouldn't really be touching the woman, but she had to check if she was breathing. There were angry red weals where the scarf had bitten in, but what caught Ally's attention most was the large red birthmark on the left side of her neck.

There didn't appear to be any pulse or breathing, but Ally knew she had to try something. She dragged Jodi gently out of the tiny space and into the main cloakroom, then began to do compressions on her chest, as she'd once been instructed during a first-aid class. Oh, how she wished she'd paid more attention, never dreaming that she'd ever have to do it!

All this time, Joyce had continued screaming, the result of which was a stampede of women all arriving on the scene.

'Has she collapsed?'

'Is she breathing?'

'Is she *dead*?'

'For God's sake,' Ally shouted as she continued to press vigorously, 'someone call the ambulance!'

Mobile phones at the ready, several of the women were doing just that. Then a small, thin woman who, according to her name badge, was Anne, offered to take over. 'I was a nurse,' she said as she relieved an already panting and grateful Ally.

Another woman crouched beside her. 'I'll take over if you get exhausted,' she said to Anne.

Ally stood up and pushed her way through the appalled cluster of women and went in search of Callum Dalrymple, the manager.

'What the hell's going on, Ally?' he asked as he headed along from the reception area. 'What's all the fuss about?'

'We need to call the police, Callum. Jodi Jones has been strangled.' Ally took his arm and led him through the door of the ladies' room.

'Oh my God!' he exclaimed as he followed Ally in and stared at the body on the floor.

'We've phoned for the ambulance,' one of the more coherent women told him. 'They say the air ambulance will be here in about half an hour and will need somewhere to land.'

Callum rubbed his forehead. 'Right, right,' he said, gathering his thoughts. 'Will any of you ladies with cars out there kindly remove them from the car park *right now* and leave them parked on the road.' He turned to Ally. 'I must speak to the other guests to get the car park cleared because I can't think of anywhere else round here where a helicopter can land easily.'

The women, many of them supporting each other, all headed obediently towards the car park. Within minutes, some other guests were streaming out and starting up their cars and, after about ten minutes, all was clear, and the women headed back into the Garden Room, chattering non-stop.

Callum re-entered the room, this time with a bottle of malt whisky and a bottle of brandy, followed by a waiter with a large tray of glasses.

'You've all had a massive shock,' he shouted through the babble of voices, 'so you'll be in need of a wee dram or something. It's on the house, so help yourselves and' – here he paused to ensure he had their attention – 'no one leaves this room. *No one*! I've called the police, and that's their orders. They'll be here shortly.'

Ally wondered how Anne was making out, but the rule applied to her too, so she concentrated on helping the women pour their drinks. Doing this gave her the opportunity to assess who'd left the Garden Room at the beginning of the break. She'd consult her list and try to add some brief descriptions to the women's names.

In the meantime, she could hear:

'Nothing to do with me! *I* never left the room!'

'Neither did I! *You* know, cos you were sitting next to me!'

'It has to be that Irish woman!'

'I hate to say it, but I really fancied that scarf.'

Anne, looking exhausted, reappeared and approached Ally. 'Barbara's taken over from me,' she said, 'but, to be honest, we're wasting our time. That woman's dead.'

Ally nodded, then, consulting her list, saw that Barbara was from Birmingham and wrote biographies. Anne, from Walsall, was a writer of women's fiction.

She then found herself included in a group of five very shaken women, all of whom insisted they had not left the room before Ally discovered Jodi's body. However, all four of her guests at the malthouse *had* been to the ladies' room at one time or another during the period in question, and so had the red-haired Della, and two others whose name badges weren't close enough to read. Ally kept hearing Della's words: 'God, I'd kill for that scarf!' But would you want the thing after you'd throttled someone with it? Probably not.

A large lady, with grey hair scraped back into a severe bun, snapped, 'Well, I've come all the way up here from Plymouth and for what? No Jodi, no course!'

'I'm so glad I went for a wee just before we came in here!' exclaimed a tiny lady with the most beautiful dark-brown eyes. Ally looked surreptitiously at her list. Anita was from Bradford and wrote about partition in India and how it had affected her family. Interesting lady.

Callum had come into the room again and made his way towards Ally. 'I cannot believe this,' he muttered to her. 'We've never had a murder in this hotel before!'

Ally patted his arm. 'Hopefully this will soon be sorted out.' She didn't really believe it would be, but she wanted to do all she could to soothe his nerves. She liked Callum. She'd known him from when she'd first arrived in Locharran and, although he was younger than her, she had rather fancied him, mainly because of his very blue Paul Newman-type eyes. That, of course, was before he began to go out with her friend, Linda, who owned The Bistro, just a few yards along the road from the hotel – and before Ally had met the lovely Ross Patterson.

That reminded her. Ross! He'd be arriving at the malthouse any minute now because she was supposed to be cooking supper for them both this evening. Ally got out her phone and began typing. *You aren't going to believe this but...*

At that moment, Ally heard the sound of the approaching helicopter. Callum rushed out, and the women all gathered round the windows to watch. It had hardly touched the ground before two paramedics were leaping out.

'Isn't this exciting!' Someone called Janine was wide-eyed. 'Just like you see on the telly! My God, girls, we've got some material here for our next books!'

Ally looked at her list. Janine came from York and wrote cosy crime.

They could all hear the sounds of chaos down the corridor in the ladies' room: feet running back and forth, doors opening and slamming, raised but calm voices calling out instructions.

After about ten minutes, a solemn-looking Callum came in again. Everyone went quiet and looked at him expectantly.

'I have to confirm,' he said, 'that Jodi Jones is indeed dead. And it appears that she has definitely been strangled. The police will be here very soon.'

There were gasps of disbelief, almost everyone looking towards Della Moran.

'Nothing to do with me!' she snapped. 'Just because I questioned her methods.'

'You went to the ladies' room!' someone shouted.

'So did plenty of other people!' Della looked around pointedly. '*You* went there, and so did *you*, and *you*...'

Ally realised that Della was pointing her finger at both Joyce and Millie.

'And so did I!' said Penelope. 'The thing is – it could have been any of us.'

Everyone looked at everyone else. Brigitte said, 'I, too, visited the ladies' room, but only to wash my hands,' in a tone that indicated this rendered her blameless.

Ally, trying to stay neutral and avoid any unpleasantness, said, 'Look, the police will be here soon, so I suggest we all have a statement ready because they'll be questioning everyone.'

It would almost certainly be poor old Rigby again. The unfortunate Detective Inspector Rigby had been persuaded by his Scottish wife to relocate from Birmingham to the Scottish Highlands, prior to his impending retirement, because 'nothing much happens up there' and, furthermore, they'd even bought a very nice wee bungalow in Inverness. Well, plenty had happened up here since Rigby's arrival, and Ally felt really sorry for him. The poor man had honestly thought he'd only be tackling the odd sheep rustler or, occasionally, a drunk at bar-closing time. That had certainly not been the case, if her recent experiences were anything to go by!

So, when Rigby and his forensic team arrived and went straight in to identify the body, Ally was quite appalled at his demeanour. The last time she'd seen him, he'd been quite robust, but he was now pale and exhausted-looking, with the appearance of someone who'd just been dragged from his bed. Ally wondered if he had, or perhaps the poor man was sickening for something?

Rigby smiled in recognition when he saw her. 'Ah, Mrs McKinley, we meet again. Tell me in detail about what you found, and when.'

She told him, with Joyce backing her up. 'We could hardly get the door of the cubicle open with her on the floor behind it.'

Rigby was taking notes and breathing deeply as if he'd just run up the hill.

He faced the room and held his hand up for silence. 'I want to talk to all the ladies who left this room at the time Miss Jones called for an interval. I realise that some of you did not, so I'll talk to *you* later.'

Ally watched as her four guests were lined up: Joyce, Millie, Penelope and Brigitte, plus Della Moran, Laura, who was a school supply teacher and wrote ghost stories, and a woman called Morwenna, who lived in Cornwall and wrote fantasy novels. They had all visited the ladies' room.

Rigby was now interviewing them, so Ally turned her attention to the five women who had not left the Garden Room. They'd be questioned, of course, but if they were telling the truth, they could hardly be held accountable. They included both Barbara and Anne who had been so helpful in trying to revive their tutor.

Half an hour passed. An ordinary ambulance arrived, and

the ladies all crowded round the window again to see Jodi's body being carried out and placed inside. In the meantime, Rigby was still intensely questioning the women who'd left the room and was looking increasingly exhausted. The helicopter was still there in the middle of the car park, rotor blades slowly turning. They obviously planned not to be around for much longer. The white-suited forensic team had gone out to the ambulance with the body, and the helicopter paramedics were now heading back towards the helicopter.

Rigby had begun to sway a little, and Ally was now alarmed; this was not the Rigby she knew! She saw him put his hand on a table to steady himself just before his eyes began to close, and he stumbled against the table before falling to the floor, causing even more mayhem among the women.

'Oh, God! Bob!' Ally realised, as she rushed to his aid, that this was the first time she'd actually called him by his Christian name. He'd always just been around, calling her 'Mrs McKinley', and she'd called him 'Inspector'. She kneeled beside him and, for the second time in as many hours, she was checking for a pulse and breathing. She couldn't find either, so she began compressions. And suddenly Anne was by her side again.

'What is it about this place?' Anne asked with a weak smile, but Ally could only hear the sound of the engine increasing as the helicopter prepared to leave.

As Anne took over again, Ally dashed towards the glass doors, where the women were gathered together waiting to see the lift-off. 'Stop them! Stop them!' she shouted as she pushed her way through to the car park. Waving her arms madly, she saw the helicopter, which had just begun to hover above the ground, land on the concrete for a second time. Within seconds, the paramedics leaped out again. 'Inside, quick!' she shouted.

She followed them inside to where Anne was still doing compressions.

'He's had a cardiac arrest!' Anne said.

'OK, we'll deal with it,' one of the paramedics said calmly, moving forward to take over the compressions while the other began unpacking the defibrillator. After a few jolts, the paramedics decided he was fit to be moved, and the more senior of the two medics shouted, 'Get a stretcher.'

Within another couple of minutes, the stretcher appeared, Rigby was loaded onto it and then rushed to the helicopter. The paramedics then jumped in themselves and, shortly after, they were up and away.

THREE

It was seven o'clock before Ally finally got back to the malthouse. Rigby had been flown away to Glasgow, to a special cardiac unit. The women attending the writers' retreat had been shepherded into the Craigmonie Hotel dining room for dinner, although most protested that they wouldn't be able to eat a thing, and Ross had arrived to take Ally home.

'Are you hungry? You have had such a shock. You really should eat something if you could face it,' he asked when, finally home, he guided her to her favourite chair beside the log burner. As she sat down, she was greeted enthusiastically by Flora, her young, black Labrador, and also by Ebony, Ross's dog, also a black Labrador, who accompanied him everywhere. To her surprise, Ally found that she was peckish, aware that her tummy was rumbling noisily. 'Do you know, I think I might just be able to manage some fish and chips?'

'Your wish is my command.' Ross picked up his jacket. 'I'll go and get some right now.' He looked at her closely. 'You sure you're OK?'

Ally shrugged wearily. 'I keep thinking about poor old Rigby. He always looked as if he had the weight of the world on his shoulders, but I'd become quite fond of him in a funny way. I hope he'll be OK.'

'He always appeared to be absolutely gobsmacked that any crime could take place up here,' Ross remarked as he made his way towards the door. 'But he should know by now that there's no getting away from the evils of this world.'

Ally wondered if he was thinking about his younger son. Not long after the Patterson family had moved up to Locharran from Glasgow forty years previously, looking for a better life, their son, Alan, had died of a drug overdose. Yes, Ross and his surviving son, Will the vet, had found a better life, but not without cost. Their son's death had also hastened that of Ross's wife a short time afterwards, as efficiently as any dagger through her heart. Ally couldn't even begin to imagine the agony of losing a child at any age, and her only prayer was that her children would survive her, as it was meant to be.

After Ross had gone out, Ally's thoughts turned to the five women who she'd welcomed to her cosy little B&B and entertained the previous night. She still couldn't get her head round the fact that there was no Jodi as she recalled their arrival the previous evening.

They'd duly arrived in Callum's people carrier at twenty minutes past six.

Ally had recognised Jodi Jones straight away, since she'd occasionally been featured in the newspapers and on television, due in no small part to her turbulent love life, and Ally had made a point of looking her up on the internet.

Jodi had a mop of greying-reddish hair and a youthful demeanour, although she had to be in her mid-sixties if she'd been to university with Desdemona, who looked a lot older. She wore a black sweater and some black leggings, but what caught

Ally's eye was the long, black-and-white silk scarf wound around her neck. She looked extremely chic.

'Now,' said Penelope Fortescue-Rawlins bossily as she led the other four women into the hallway of The Auld Malthouse, 'I hope we're happy about who's sharing with who? Jodi's having Room One on her own; Brigitte, you're sharing with me, and Millie and Joyce, you'll be sharing the third room.'

'Yes, yes,' they confirmed in unison, having heard it all before. They insisted that they could manage to carry their own suitcases, and Ally led the way upstairs, opening the door of Room 1 for Jodi, and then opening the doors of Rooms 2 and 3 for the other four to sort themselves out. She informed them that she'd be doing a light, informal supper in her kitchen – leaving the dining room pristine for the serving of breakfast the following morning – at around half past seven for any of them who wanted to join. For the rest of the retreat, they would eat their lunch and dinner at the Craigmonie, but Ally had made some pasta, assuming they'd be too tired after their long journeys to go back down there again.

As Ally made her way towards the stairs, she was waylaid by Jodi. '*Love* the room!' she said. 'And this supper idea is so very kind of you. These ladies have come from all over the country; from London, Kent and Gloucestershire, and even Northern Ireland on this occasion, so they've been travelling for most of the day. And they're not exactly in their *first flush of youth*! That applies to me too because I've driven up from South Wales and I'm truly knackered.'

Ally returned to the kitchen to let them settle in and to make a large bowl of salad to go with the vegetarian pasta she'd put together earlier.

The first duo to arrive in the kitchen were the two women who were sharing Room 3.

'Hello,' said the taller of the two. 'I'm Joyce Williams, and this is Millie.'

'Millie Day,' said the smaller of the two, almost apologetically. 'Short for Camilla.'

'Very regal,' Ally said, laughing, although regal was not an adjective she'd have used to describe Millie.

They were polar opposites. Joyce was a big-built woman and probably in her mid-sixties, Ally reckoned, who seemed supremely self-confident. Millie, on the other hand, with her salt-and-pepper hair and hesitant manner, was short and sturdily built.

Joyce raved about the kitchen. 'This is so spacious, yet cosy,' she proclaimed, looking around approvingly at Ally's painted wooden units, at the Aga, the log burner, and the long wooden table set for six.

'I know it's unusual to have an Aga and a log burner in one room,' Ally said, 'but the Aga is oil-fired and provides all the central heating and hot water. And when I spotted the big old inglenook, I just knew I *had* to have a log burner.' *And I'm still paying for it*, Ally thought.

'Could I please ask you a favour?' Joyce asked.

'Yes, of course,' Ally replied, wondering what was coming.

'I'm diabetic and I really need somewhere to store my insulin,' Joyce asked, looking worried. 'I wondered if I could store it in your refrigerator?'

'No problem,' Ally said. 'I have an enormous fridge and there's plenty of room. Just remind me every day and I'll bring it out for you. I'll store it all in a big Tupperware box and stick a "Joyce" label on it.' She made a mental note to buy some small fridges for the bedrooms so that her guests could access ice cubes, wines and milk, not to mention any medication they might have.

Millie, who'd been looking around silently, came alive as

Flora came bounding in from outside. 'What's your dog called?' she asked.

'That's Flora,' Ally told her, watching the little woman stroke the dog and play with her silky ears.

Just then, Brigitte and Penelope appeared.

'Hello, I'm Brigitte.' Brigitte was plainly French, pretty with large brown eyes and her hair tied up in a carefully careless chignon, and much younger than the others.

'And I'm Penelope,' said the last of the four. 'I'm the leader and organiser of The Literary Ladies, and I've come all the way up from the Cotswolds,' Penelope said very loudly in her very posh accent. She had a double-barrelled surname, which Ally had not yet memorised. She wasn't exactly chinless but wasn't too strong in that department, with short greying hair and sharp blue eyes. 'This is so kind of you, Mrs McKinley,' she bellowed.

'Please, everyone, do call me Ally, and do help yourselves to a glass of wine.' She indicated the dresser. 'I've opened a few bottles, but I have to warn you that this is nothing fancy, just supermarket red.'

'Suits me,' boomed Penelope, leading the way, with Brigitte and Millie eagerly following.

'I don't drink alcohol,' Joyce said, 'because I'm diabetic, but I'd love a sparkling water or something.'

It was a good ten minutes later before Jodi swanned in, wearing what looked like her pyjamas but was probably some form of leisurewear. She was wearing another beautiful long silk scarf around her neck, this one in what could only be described as shocking pink.

'Sorry I'm a bit late,' she said breathlessly, 'but I've had a long chat with my agent on the phone.' She rolled her eyes. 'You *know* what these agents are like!'

The others obviously didn't because no one uttered a word.

'Please sit down, everyone,' Ally said, lifting the pasta dish out of the oven, 'and help yourself to wine, Jodi.'

As they took their places around the table, Joyce said, 'This is so very kind of you, Ally.'

There was a general nodding of heads.

'This is so much nicer than some dreary hotel,' Jodi said, helping herself to garlic bread and taking a hefty gulp of her red wine.

'But you'd probably be having a nice three-course dinner down at the Craigmonie,' Ally said. 'The food is really very good there.'

'Who needs a three-course dinner?' shouted Penelope, followed by murmurs of agreement. 'A quick supper and an early night.'

'Well,' said Joyce, 'I have some good news, which I haven't told anyone else yet. I've just had *another* short story published by a women's magazine, and that's *four* now!'

'Congratulations,' said Penelope without enthusiasm.

'That's wonderful,' said Brigitte drily.

Millie cleared her throat. 'What do you write about, Joyce? I don't recall reading any of your stories.'

'Women!' said Joyce. 'Women like us. Ordinary women. You should read the popular women's magazines, Millie.'

There was silence as everyone ate and digested this news.

Then Jodi said, 'Have you ever considered sexing them up a little, Joyce?'

'Ooh la la!' said Brigitte, rolling her eyes.

'We don't *all* want to read erotica,' snapped Joyce. This was an obvious dig back at Jodi, who wrote very racy, explicit novels.

Perhaps sensing some dissension, Millie interjected quickly with, 'How long have you lived here, Ally?'

'About a year and a half,' Ally replied. 'I come from Edinburgh and lived there most of my life. I was widowed about nine years ago, my son and daughter are both married with families of their own, and I decided to make a new start.'

'Wow!' exclaimed Jodi. 'That was so brave! Especially at your age!'

Slightly annoyed, Ally said, 'Perhaps, but I see no reason why older women shouldn't do something with their lives if they want to, and they're fit enough, that is. I fell in love with this old building, originally a store for the malt that makes the local whisky, mainly because of its position in the hills, with the castle towering above and the village alongside the river below.'

'What about the famous earl?' asked Penelope loudly. 'We were all mates at uni, you know, and my late husband was a friend of his.'

'Hamish is actually a very good friend of mine,' Ally said staunchly. 'He's recently remarried, and his wife is expecting twins.'

'Have you ever thought about marrying again, Ally?' Millie asked timidly.

'Well, no, I haven't,' Ally said, feeling rather self-conscious, 'but I have met someone new since coming up here.'

'Oh, *do* tell us more!' Joyce urged. 'The love lives of older women provides such good material for my short stories.'

'Well,' said Ally, 'his name is Ross Patterson and he's supposedly a retired vet, but he spends half his "retirement" standing in for his son, also a vet, who inherited the business from his father.'

'Good for you, Ally – love is love whatever your age,' said Brigitte enthusiastically.

The pasta was a great success, and everyone, except Jodi, had second helpings. And everyone, including Jodi, was on their second or third glass of wine. Supermarket brand or not, it was going down well. The ladies were all beginning to visibly droop though.

Millie was the first to crumble. 'That was lovely,' she said, 'but I'm utterly exhausted. It's been a long day. Will you excuse me?'

Joyce stood up. 'I'll come too, so I don't disturb you later. I'm knackered anyway.'

Penelope yawned. 'And so say all of us.'

Brigitte gave a Gallic shrug. 'OK, so it is bedtime.'

'What time would you like me to serve breakfast?' Ally asked as they began to make their way towards the stairs.

Jodi stood up and looked around at them all. 'Our schedule states that we have breakfast at nine thirty, then we go down to the hotel to meet up with the other ladies and have lunch at twelve thirty. At three o'clock I will give a lecture for about an hour and a half.' She paused and turned to Ally. 'Ally, I would like to thank you for your kindness this evening and would be honoured if you could join us tomorrow afternoon – just so you can see what this little group is all about.'

Put that way, how could Ally have refused?

Now, as she remembered that previous evening, Ally could scarcely believe that today had ended the way it had. Who would do such a thing? A horrible thought crossed her mind. Could the murderer be one of the ladies, her ladies, right here in The Auld Malthouse?

FOUR

When Ross returned with the fish and chips, he asked, 'Where are your guests now?'

Ally shrugged. 'They're probably having their dinner at the hotel; that's if any of them are particularly hungry after finding Jodi strangled and the detective inspector having a heart attack.'

'Enough excitement for one day I should think,' Ross agreed. 'Any idea who might have strangled that Josie?'

'Jodi,' Ally corrected. 'Jodi Jones. A very successful writer of women's fiction, accused of plagiarism by a fiery Irish lady who just happened to be sitting next to me.'

'And who, I suppose, must therefore be the obvious suspect?'

Ally nodded. 'According to Callum, for some of the so-called coffee break, Jodi was in the bar, downing a hefty Scotch, before she went to the ladies' room. The thing is, nobody in the bar paid much attention to who visited the ladies' room and for how long – because you don't, do you?'

'No, I don't suppose you do,' Ross agreed, shaking his head.

'All four staying here went to the ladies' room at some time during the break, but not all together, of course! And then there was Della, the Irish lady. They're all suspects now, and they got questioned rather thoroughly. I just wonder how much information Rigby got before he hit the floor.'

Ross looked thoughtful. 'Don't forget there were other guests in the hotel. It *could* be someone else.'

'I suppose it could be.' Ally sighed. 'God only knows what happens now.'

After they'd eaten and had a glass of wine, Ross said, 'And now you're going to tell me that you want to stay up until your guests come back?'

Ally nodded. 'What else can I do, Ross? It would seem heartless to just let them come in and go straight up to their rooms. I was thinking of shepherding them into the sitting room and offering them a hot drink or something.'

'Even though one of them might be the killer?'

'Even though one of them might be the killer...'

'That night of passion I envisaged is rapidly fading,' Ross said with a sigh.

'Never mind,' Ally said soothingly, patting his hand. 'They do say that anticipation can sometimes be the best part...'

The four women returned not long before ten o'clock. Brigitte and Penelope had driven up from the south, and still had their cars parked in the village, whereas Millie had made the journey by air to Inverness, and then by bus. Joyce, who didn't drink and who had a large Range Rover, had driven them back up to the malthouse.

'It was parked out on the road anyway because of having to clear the car park,' she said, 'and I wanted to bring it up here.'

Ally ushered them into the large sitting room and offered hot drinks and/or nightcaps.

'I'd love a hot chocolate!' exclaimed Joyce.

'Great idea,' the other three chorused.

'We've had such a load of alcohol this afternoon and evening,' Penelope said cheerfully. 'But we bloody well needed it, didn't we, gals?'

The 'gals', apart from Joyce, all agreed that they had indeed needed alcohol after the horrendous events of the afternoon.

'So now there is no Jodi,' Brigitte said sadly.

'To be honest, I didn't like her that much,' Joyce admitted. 'I must confess that I wasn't particularly shocked when Della came up with the plagiarism thing because I think she stole one of my ideas too...'

'What makes you think that?' Penelope asked.

'Because one of her plots was very similar to one of mine which I'd sent for her to edit,' Joyce replied.

'No smoke without fire, I suppose,' Penelope said brusquely.

'And this course has cost a lot of money, so what happens now?' Millie asked.

'We are not giving up now, ladies!' Penelope said loudly. 'You've paid for a course, and I shall *give you* a course.'

'But what would we do?' Millie asked.

'Well, we can still do writing exercises and brainstorming sessions.'

'But we should discuss how Jodi died and who could have possibly done it. Surely that would be a good base for crime stories?' Ally suggested hopefully.

Penelope guffawed. 'Obviously there's little doubt that the Irish woman killed her,' she said firmly in her usual loud fashion.

'That's true; after all, if it wasn't any of us, who else could it be?' Millie asked.

'It could have been that Laura whatever-her-name-is,' Joyce said. 'I thought she was a bit strange, and I thought all along that she had another agenda.' She put her head in her hands. 'Oh God, I'm never going to forget seeing Jodi lying there...'

'If only we hadn't needed the toilet,' Millie said sadly.

'Some of us *have* to go!' Penelope boomed. 'I have a very weak bladder, I'll have you know.'

'Have you tried those special pants they keep advertising?' asked Joyce, who seemed more than happy to change the subject.

Ally decided this was a good time to escape to the kitchen and make the hot chocolates.

'This is Ross,' Ally announced as he followed her into the sitting room a little while later, carefully carrying a large tray of hot chocolates, followed by two excited Labradors. As she shooed them back into the kitchen, Ally was aware that he was being scrutinised and was also aware of some muted murmurs of approval. And so there should be, she thought. Ross was tall, lean, silver haired and blue eyed, and he looked very tasty this evening. Pity about the night of passion though, but Ally couldn't imagine either of them staying awake long enough for anything other than a hasty goodnight kiss.

'That policeman said he wanted us to stay here,' Brigitte said, stirring her drink. 'So now we must be here for some time and my husband will go crazy!'

'Do you know how long for?' Millie asked, looking horrified.

Brigitte shrugged again. 'I do not know.'

'What will happen,' boomed Penelope, 'is that most likely we will have to stay here until someone is arrested, and that's *that!*'

'But,' Joyce said, 'the detective is presumably in hospital, if he's still alive, and so who takes over? And when will the new detective, he or she, get here? And will we have to answer all those questions and give new statements all over again?'

There were groans all round before Brigitte stood up and drained her mug. 'I am going to bed. Thank you so much, Ally. And, Ross,' she added, giving him a coy little smile.

This was followed by a great deal of yawning and mug-draining and the other three decided it was time to go to bed too. Ally could hear them talking as they made their way upstairs.

'What a day!'

'What happens now?'

'Do we get our money back?'

Shortly after they'd all disappeared upstairs and Ross had kindly stacked the dishwasher, switched it on and let the dogs out for ten minutes, they too made their way upstairs, to Ally's room.

'Who do you think is a likely killer?' she asked Ross as she got into bed.

'Let me clean my teeth and we'll have a chat about it in bed,' Ross replied.

But by the time Ross had finished in the bathroom and climbed into bed, Ally was already fast asleep.

FIVE

In the morning, Ally's four remaining guests all arrived in the dining room within ten minutes of each other, and seemed uncharacteristically quiet as they helped themselves to fruit and cereals. Penelope and Millie both opted for cooked breakfasts today, while both Joyce and Brigitte confessed to being 'not very hungry'. Ally could understand that as she had very little appetite herself.

'So, what's our schedule for today then?' Joyce asked no one in particular as Ally served the cooked breakfasts.

There followed much headshaking and shrugging.

'Well,' said Penelope loudly, 'we still must go to the hotel for lunch and dinner, and I suggest that we try to follow the original schedule as closely as possible, even if Jodi is not around to critique our work.'

'Perhaps we could mark each other's?' Millie suggested quietly.

'I have decided,' Penelope said loudly and firmly, 'that each of us will tell our life story, or talk about incidents in our life, every morning. Then, in the afternoons, we can compose a short story based on what we heard. We can then read them out and, as Millie suggests, critique each other's writing.'

There were some moans in the background.

'I'm not happy standing up and talking to people,' Joyce muttered. She looked unsure and uncomfortable, and Ally wondered why.

'All I can think of is my life in France before I met my husband,' Brigitte said.

'I'm not very interesting,' Millie said, 'although I did once, long ago, almost get chosen for the Olympics.'

'That's amazing!' Joyce exclaimed.

'I would love to hear about that,' Brigitte said.

'Good, good! That's settled then,' boomed Penelope. 'Brilliant idea! We'll go ahead with that then.'

No one argued.

'My husband will arrive here tomorrow,' Brigitte said to Ally. 'Can we talk later?'

Ally nodded, having a fair idea what might be coming. She could hear the phone ringing in the hall and Ross answering it. When she returned to the kitchen, Ross said, 'That was the police.'

'Did they say how Rigby was?' Ally asked anxiously.

'He's still alive, but they didn't have an update on his progress,' Ross said. 'His replacement on this case is on his way and wants to talk to you before he interviews the women at the hotel. Incidentally, he wants *all* the women to be at the Craigmonie today, including the four who're staying here.'

'They planned to go down there anyway,' Ally said. She sighed loudly. 'This is so crazy! I have no idea for how long these women will be here, what they're going to be doing, or how many husbands and partners are likely to appear. Just as well I haven't any more bookings for another month or so.' This reminded her of Brigitte, who was still presumably waiting in the dining room.

But Brigitte wasn't in the dining room, so Ally ventured upstairs and, as she walked past Jodi's room, noticed that the door was ajar. She was sure she'd left it closed, and she'd meant to lock it because she knew the police might want to look in there but had been distracted by the other guests returning as she'd been looking for the key.

Ally opened the door and there, standing in front of the chest of drawers reading what looked like a diary, was none other than Brigitte.

Brigitte laid the diary down hastily. 'I just wanted to have a look at the room,' she said, 'because I wondered if I could move in here when my husband arrives tomorrow? He worries about me, you see?' She gave a little pout. 'Now that Jodi is no longer here, is it possible we could move in here, with the double bed?' She looked sadly at Ally. 'Also, I do not like to tell her, but that Penelope snores *like a hippopotamus*! So *loud*. I cannot *sleep*.'

Ally had never heard a hippopotamus snore, but since Penelope was so loud anyway, she didn't doubt it for a moment. 'I have every sympathy, Brigitte, but the new detective is on his way now to talk to us all, and for sure he's going to want to check Jodi's room. And she has a husband who will doubtless want to deal with her personal things. So perhaps we can talk about it again tomorrow?'

Brigitte pulled a face but nodded. 'Yes, of course. And I must tell you that there were some strange noises coming from our bathroom also on Sunday night, which I think is perhaps the pipes, but it was difficult to know because of the snoring.'

'Oh dear,' said Ally.

Oh, Willie! she thought.

Wailing Willie was the ghost she'd acquired along with the malthouse. A couple of hundred years ago, Willie, along with his bagpipes, had broken into the still-functioning malthouse to taste some of the finished product, also stored there, and had happily drunk himself to death while playing his pipes. The drunker Willie got, the more wailing emanated from the pipes, and now, rumour had it, Willie still wailed away shortly before a local death was imminent.

Ally, originally sceptical, was now more inclined to admit that there just might be *some* truth in this after some of the events which had occurred over the past year. If Willie was still around, he inhabited the en-suite bathroom to Room 2.

But as she made her way downstairs, Ally wasn't thinking about Willie; she kept visualising Brigitte standing in Room 1 reading Jodi's diary. It was high time the bedroom door was locked, so she went straight downstairs, got the key, and did just that.

Morag McConnachie arrived at nine o'clock to do the cleaning. As she tied her apron round her middle, she said, 'For God's sake, Ally, what's goin' on in Locharran?'

'One of my guests was murdered at the Craigmonie yesterday afternoon – *that's* what's going on,' Ally replied somewhat tersely.

Morag stared at her. 'There was police all over the place this mornin',' she said, 'and the Craigmonie's not takin' any new guests for the moment.'

'The police will have to examine everything thoroughly before it can be opened up again, I expect.'

'But, Ally, who *was* she? And how did she get hersel' murdered?'

'I don't think she planned it exactly, Morag! She was an author, giving a lecture, and later found strangled in the ladies' toilet – by *me!*'

'It was yersel' that found her?' Morag stared at her in horror. 'Oh my God! Ye couldnae make it up.'

Never was a truer word spoken, Ally thought.

After the four women had left in Joyce's Land Rover, and

Morag was vacuuming upstairs, the inevitable happened. It was her son on the phone.

'Mum!' Jamie said. 'I've just seen the news. You've got *another* murder!'

'I'm afraid so,' Ally admitted.

'You once said that you wanted to get away from the crime of the big city,' Jamie said to her sternly, 'and look where it's got you. This is ridiculous! You must really think about selling up that place and coming back to civilisation.'

Ally rolled her eyes. 'Honestly, Jamie, I'm fine. Really. And I love it here.'

'If it wasn't for the fact I know you've got Ross living nearby,' he said, 'I'd be right up there to bring you back. I worry about you.'

'You've no need to,' Ally assured him as she ended the call. 'I'm well looked after.' She was perfectly aware that Jamie, no matter how concerned he might be, would find it difficult to abandon his building company even for a day or two. Likewise his wife, Liz, with her boutique.

Her thoughts were interrupted by a knock at the door, which made Ally worry in case it might be a guest seeking accommodation and she wouldn't be able to accommodate them.

On the doorstep was a tall, very good-looking South Asian man. He looked as if he might be in his mid-forties. He was smiling, and he had lovely teeth. Ally was very fussy about teeth, and his were beautiful.

'Can I help you?' she asked. 'I'm afraid all my rooms are taken at the moment...'

He held up his ID card. 'Detective Inspector Amir Kandahar,' he said in a broad Glaswegian accent.

'Oh!' Ally was momentarily at a loss for words. With everything else going on, she'd forgotten that Rigby's replacement was on his way. 'Oh, do come in,' she added hastily and led the way into the guests' sitting room, cursing the fact she hadn't removed last night's mugs from the coffee table. 'I hope you don't mind these,' she said, waving her hand at the mugs. 'I haven't had time to tidy up. My guests had hot chocolates when they got back last night.'

'That's quite all right,' he said, smiling again as he took a seat. 'I'm sorry to bother you when you're obviously busy, but I do have to ask you about yesterday afternoon at the Craigmonie Hotel. Detective Inspector Rigby obviously recorded a lot of conversation before he—'

'How is he?' Ally interrupted anxiously as she sat down opposite him. 'Have you heard anything?'

'He's in Glasgow Royal Infirmary and making good progress. I went to see him for a few minutes when he got there last night, and he said that I should see you first because it was you who found the body of Jodi Jones. He also said it was you who saved his life as well.'

'Do you think he'll be able to return to work any time soon?' Ally asked.

'It seems unlikely that he'll be back in harness for quite a while, so I'm taking over for the moment.'

'Poor Rigby,' Ally said sadly.

'I'm afraid you'll have to make do with me for the time being,' he said, displaying that lovely smile again. 'Now, I must ask you about yesterday afternoon.'

Ally tried to pull her thoughts together. She began to tell him about the ladies' writing retreat and how she'd agreed to sit in on the afternoon session. She told him about the fiery, red-haired Irish lady who had caused mayhem by accusing the famous Jodi Jones of plagiarism, and the coffee break that immediately followed it, when some of the women went to the ladies' room and some didn't. Finally, she told that, when Jodi failed to reappear, she and Joyce went to investigate her whereabouts. 'And I found her on the floor, right behind the cubicle door, her scarf pulled like a ligature around her neck. It was Joyce screaming that alerted all the other ladies, who came rushing to the scene.'

'You attempted resuscitation?' he asked.

'Yes, but I'm not very practiced at it so, when another lady at the retreat called Anne offered to take over, I was very relieved. She said she'd been a nurse.'

The inspector nodded. 'And it looked to you as if the ligature was the victim's own scarf?'

'Yes, that's why I had to loosen it. And we'd all remarked about how lovely it was – the scarf, I mean!' Ally said, feeling a little embarrassed at her choice of words, even as she shuddered at the memory.

'So someone had bound this tightly round her neck,' he stated.

'It was awful, Inspector. Her face was all red, and there were scratch marks where she'd tried to pull the scarf away...'

'Yes, I've seen the body, Mrs McKinley, and the pathology report indicates there's no doubt she was strangled by someone who exerted great force, great strength. In your opinion, would you say that any of the women are particularly strong?'

'Well, I suppose either Joyce or Penelope could fit the bill. Or it could, of course, have been a guest from another part of the hotel,' Ally said.

'Mr Dalrymple thinks that's very unlikely, since that whole area was cordoned off for the writers' group,' Amir said. 'Are there any of the other women who you think might be a likely suspect?'

Ally shook her head. 'I hardly know them,' she said. 'But I suppose you can never tell.'

'You're right, you can never tell. I shall be interviewing them all this afternoon.'

'Would you like some tea or coffee, Inspector?' Ally asked,

remembering Rigby who never turned down the offer of a cup of tea and used to eat all her shortbread.

'That's a kind offer,' he said, 'but I've a lot to do this morning, so I'm afraid I must refuse.' He cocked his head to one side, listening. 'Is there someone upstairs?'

'Yes, that's my cleaner, Morag McConnachie. I don't know what I'd do without her when I have guests. She's a brilliant cleaner. Her husband, Murdo, is the postman here.' *And a source of gossip for miles around*, she refrained from adding.

'She wouldn't have been anywhere around yesterday afternoon?' he asked.

'No, she only comes here for a few hours in the morning when I have guests,' Ally replied. 'I've warned her not to go into Room One. That's the room Jodi occupied until yesterday.'

He stood up. 'Would you mind if I examine her bedroom now?' he asked.

'Not at all, Inspector,' Ally said, getting to her feet. 'I locked it up because I suspected you'd want to do that. One of my guests is expecting her husband to join her soon and has asked if she can move into that room, so the sooner you can give me the all-clear, so much the better.'

'Well, the deceased's husband is also on his way, and I think we should give him some priority, don't you?'

'I do,' Ally agreed.

'I understand that Detective Inspector Rigby thought very highly of you as the local sleuth,' he said, smiling again.

Ally was astounded. 'But he always doubted *everything* I said...'

'That's what police do!' said his stand-in. 'As you know the area so well, I might need you to work with me on this, but for the moment, could you just direct me to Miss Jones's room, please?'

As Ally led the way upstairs, still trying to digest what the inspector had just said, she encountered Morag and the vacuum cleaner on the landing, staring open-mouthed at the handsome visitor.

'This is Detective Inspector Kandahar, Morag,' she explained, 'who's come to check out Room One.'

Morag nodded wordlessly as Ally unlocked the door and ushered the detective in.

'I'll leave you to it then, Inspector,' she said.

'Thank you, and please call me Amir,' he said.

'In which case I'm Ally.'

He'd hardly gone through the door before the phone rang again. This time it was her daughter Carol calling from Wiltshire.

'Mum, what on earth's going on in that village of yours?'

Ally sighed. 'Yes, very unfortunate.'

'*Unfortunate?* Mum, you could be in danger. I know we've had this conversation before, but I really mean it! Look, we have a lovely spare room, with an en suite and everything, so why don't you come down for a few weeks and let them all get on with it?'

'You're very kind, darling. But I have the remaining ladies staying here, and I'm running a business, like it or not. Anyway, I've got Ross with me a great deal of the time, and I feel safe with him.'

'You could bring him down too. It's a double bed. I shouldn't say that, should I? Dad would probably spin in his grave!'

Ally smiled. 'I don't think Dad would. I think he'd most likely be pleased for me. But, Carol, double bed and en suite or not, I'm *not* coming. I can't at the moment anyway, but it's kind of you to worry about me.'

'You're my *mum*!' Carol exclaimed. 'Of course I worry about you. If it wasn't for the kids, I'd be right up there.'

'Absolutely no need,' Ally said firmly. 'And I think this will be solved quite quickly.'

She only hoped she was right.

SIX

Morag untied the pinny from around her ample curves, wiped her brow and sat down with a cup of tea in the kitchen, as she did every morning when she'd finished doing the bedrooms. She was a small, plump woman of sixty with permed, not-very-well-dyed greying hair and bright-blue eyes.

'Well I never!' exclaimed Morag. 'A detective.'

'He seems really nice,' Ally said, listening out for her new friend coming down the stairs. Then, aware of footsteps on the stairs, she said, 'Excuse me for a minute, Morag.'

She met Amir in the hallway, where he handed her back the key to Room 1.

'I'll let the husband clear her personal effects,' he said, 'when he arrives tonight.'

Ally nodded as she showed him towards the door.

'I've no doubt our paths will be crossing from time to time,' he said, bestowing her with another dazzling smile. 'Thanks for your cooperation today, Ally,' he added.

Ally smiled. 'It's been a pleasure, Amir.'

Back in the kitchen, Ally replaced the key to Room 1 in the drawer of the dresser.

'He called ye *Ally*!' Morag exclaimed.

'Well, that's my name,' Ally replied. 'And I called him *Amir*.' She poured herself a cup of tea, still reeling with the shock that Rigby had considered her to be a 'good sleuth' – Rigby, who'd questioned and doubted everything she'd ever suggested on previous occasions. Did Amir think she was some sort of expert then? She'd hate to disillusion him. And they'd already got on to first name terms, unlike Rigby, who had always called her Mrs McKinley.

'Well I never!' Morag repeated, draining her mug. 'Wait till I tell Murdo.'

At that moment, Ally spotted the husband, Murdo, with his shiny bald head and prolific white moustache. He had just pulled up outside in his little red van.

'Murdo's arrived,' Ally said.

'Oh, tell him to come in,' Morag said eagerly, plainly desperate to impart this latest piece of information.

Murdo didn't need much persuading because he often stopped for a cup of tea on his postal rounds.

'Phew! It's warm today,' he exclaimed as he came into the kitchen and handed a bunch of letters to Ally. He looked at his wife. 'Ye're still here then?'

'Ye wait until ye hear what I have to tell ye, Murdo McConnachie,' Morag shouted at him. 'We've had a visit from the *new detective*!'

'Oh aye? I heard all about some woman bein' killed and that Rigby was in hospital. So, what's he like?' Murdo accepted his mug of tea and helped himself to a chocolate biscuit, completely unfazed by Morag's excitement.

'*My* goodness, he's an awful lot younger and better lookin' than Rigby,' proclaimed Morag triumphantly. 'And he cannae be more than twenty-somethin'.'

Ally sighed. 'Morag, I think he must be in his forties, but he is very good-looking.'

'And he's callin' her *Ally*!' Morag continued. 'And she's callin' him *Amour*! I thought that meant "*love*".'

'*Amir*,' Ally corrected. 'He's a charming man who's taken over from Rigby for the moment.'

'Well I never!' said Murdo, gulping down his tea and obviously eager to be off to spread this gem all around the village. 'Well I never!'

As soon as Morag and Murdo had departed, Ally decided she needed to have a look in Room 1 while the house was empty and to see what Brigitte had been looking at. She made her way upstairs.

There was no sign of the diary. Had Amir taken it? She looked around and then moved the chest of drawers slightly forward. And there was the diary! It had slipped down the back of the chest, so Amir had obviously missed it.

On picking it up, Ally realised that it was marked by a ribbon for this particular week, but the page for the first four days had been torn out. Why? On closer inspection, she could see the indent of Jodi's heavy-handed writing on the previous page. She could just decipher 'meeting with Brigitte'. So, Jodi should have been having a meeting with Brigitte on that very day! Why would she be doing that? And had Jodi torn the pages out herself for some reason, or had Brigitte done so? What did it mean?

Ally wondered for a moment what to do. Then, slipping the diary into her pocket, she decided to hang on to it and show it to Amir when she next saw him.

Locharran Village Post Office and General Stores was run by two elderly spinster sisters, Queenie and Bessie MacDougall.

They'd taken over from their parents fifty years ago, and, by the look of things, not a great deal had changed since.

Ally had no doubt that this would have been Murdo's first port of call because, Queenie, in particular, was the centre of all village gossip. She spent her time permanently hunched across the counter in an effort to see and hear everything that could be going on and that might otherwise escape her notice.

So when Ally arrived in the shop later that day to buy some milk, she found Queenie typically misinformed.

'I hear they're havin' to bring the *pollis* in from *India* now!' Queenie said, by way of greeting.

'I'd hazard a guess that he's come all the way from Glasgow,' Ally said. 'And he's extremely nice. I'll take two pints of milk, if you please, Queenie.'

'Milk fer Mrs McKinley,' Queenie bawled at Bessie who, as usual, was unpacking boxes and stocking shelves. 'And what about this poor woman at the Craigmonie?' she continued. 'Strangled when she went for a pee! Ye canna go anywhere and be safe thae days.' She looked hard at Ally. 'And it wiz yersel' what found her!'

'I'm afraid so,' Ally admitted.

'Well, well, well!' said Queenie, plainly momentarily at a loss for words. 'And I'm hearin' that ye're right pally with him and callin' him *Amour*! What's yer boyfriend goin' to think of that, eh?'

'Amir,' Ally corrected. '*Amir*. Nothing whatsoever to do with love!' Although, she thought privately, he *was* extremely dishy.

'Yer milk, Mrs McKinley,' said Bessie, who was clad in her normal uniform of ancient jumper and droopy skirt that barely concealed her billowing underwear. Ally had often wondered who bought these old-fashioned knickers, elasticated just above the knee. Now she knew.

. . .

Ally had just got home when she had another visitor. She wasn't surprised to see Desdemona arrive because she had called her the previous evening to tell her of the death of her friend but hadn't been able to get through. And it was too delicate a subject to impart in a voicemail.

'What the hell's going on?' Desdemona asked as, without preamble, she marched in through the door. 'I heard it on the *news*! My friend Jodi!'

Desdemona was a little odd, no two ways about that, but she was a brilliant painter. Then again, her entire family had been a little odd, according to local legend. Her father had been a professor of English, her mother an actress. Nobody knew what had brought them and their two daughters – Desdemona and Ophelia – up from London to this remote highland region, to the isolated house on the side of Loch Trioch. The professor had constructed a large, walled garden, where Desdemona, now the only survivor of the family, still grew exotic herbs, spices and vegetables, which she sold in the village from time to time.

Now she plonked herself down on a kitchen chair, in a colourful flurry of violently patterned kaftan with purple beads and purple leggings, and patted an enthusiastically welcoming Flora.

Ally nodded as she began to make coffee. 'I'm really sorry you had to find out that way, Desdemona, as I know she was your friend. I tried calling you last night, but you didn't pick up. It's a real tragedy.' She could see Desdemona's eyes were full of tears.

Desdemona dabbed her eyes. 'Who, in God's name, would do such a thing? And *why?*'

'Well,' said Ally, clearing her throat, 'I have to tell you that she was accused of plagiarism publicly by one of the women, and then one of the other women, who's staying here, has said much the same thing. I've no idea if that was the reason for her murder but must admit it seems a bit extreme. Remind me how you like your coffee?'

'Black, please.' Desdemona leaned forward. 'There are only a few things that really cause people to kill, and having a silly story copied is not one of them! There'll be far more to it than that, you mark my words. Love, hate, jealousy, revenge – take your pick.'

'I daresay you're right,' Ally said, handing her a mug of coffee, 'but without knowing these women's histories, it would be difficult to pinpoint.'

'That's what the bloody police are supposed to be doing!' snapped Desdemona, gulping some coffee. 'Solving crime. Not farting about checking on vehicle MOTs and car tax.'

'Have you sorted yours out yet?' Ally asked, gazing out of the window at the mud-covered decrepit old Land Rover parked outside.

'I damn well *had* to! Rigby got on to me. Gave me twenty-four hours to get it all sorted out or he'd be informing the authorities.'

'Well, at least he gave you time to get it put right. *Poor* old Rigby,' Ally said sadly. 'Did you hear that he had a heart attack?'

'Good Lord! Did he die?' Desdemona asked.

'Fortunately not,' Ally replied.

'So who do we have *now*?'

'Detective Inspector Amir Kandahar,' Ally said. 'He's a Glaswegian and very charming, and he appears to be very much on the ball.'

Desdemona looked unconvinced. 'Like I said, he needs to begin by checking on these women's backgrounds just for a start.'

'I'm expecting a visit from Jodi's husband,' Ally said. 'He's coming to collect her things, I believe.'

Desdemona snorted. 'Bloody Owen! Him and his self-built shack in the woods! Jodi wasn't having *that*!'

'Did she leave then?' Ally asked.

'Oh yes, long time ago. She's had several lovers, has Jodi, but she's been with the same man now for a number of years. But, of course, Owen's still legally her husband I think, so I suppose he'll inherit all her worldly goods, the bastard. Makes me sick! And he's having it off with someone else I'm told.'

'Well, you can hardly blame him if Jodi was doing the same thing.'

'I just hope that Jodi thought to make a will and keep him out of it.'

Ally didn't reply for a moment, knowing full well that he'd most likely be able to claim anyway, but it was best not to agitate Desdemona any further. 'So he's having an affair then?'

'An *affair*! It's all "free love" in his woodland paradise! Everyone shagging everyone else!' Desdemona drained her coffee. 'He'd be a definite suspect if you ask me.'

'But he's not arrived yet!' Ally said, staring at her.

'So far as you know,' Desdemona said, standing up. 'He could be hiding away somewhere for all we know, and he could have sneaked into the hotel and killed poor Jodi.'

'I doubt he could have got into the ladies' room at exactly the right moment, strangled her and then left without being seen or bumping into one of the women,' Ally remarked.

'I wouldn't put it past him, slimy bugger. Just hope your Glaswegian detective is on the ball. Keep me informed, will you?'

Ally nodded as she accompanied Desdemona to the door. It was after Desdemona had left that Ally realised she should have questioned her about being at university with Jodi. She'd appreciate more information about Jodi Jones.

.   .   .

'Della wants to move up here to stay with you,' Joyce informed her later when the women came back in the late afternoon. 'She says all the other women are horrible to her and she's being ostracised.'

Rightly or wrongly, Della was, of course, the chief suspect, and Ally couldn't help but feel a little sorry for her. She'd have liked to be able to offer Della a room but, she wondered, what was to stop her own four guests treating her in exactly the same way? Particularly as they'd want to exonerate themselves. And anyway, Brigitte had asked first.

'He's good-looking though, that new detective,' piped up Millie.

'Yes, he is indeed,' Ally agreed, trying to change the subject. 'So, who had to talk about their lives today? I gather you're doing life story sharing as part of the revised course?'

'None other than Penelope herself!' Joyce said. 'She wittered on for a good hour about how brilliant she was with horses. Catching horses, riding horses, showing horses, horses jumping, horses racing, dressage – you name it! Horses, horses, bloody horses! How can you write a love story about a horse, for God's sake?'

'Perhaps it could be about a lady of the manor falling in love with a stable hand?' Ally suggested.

Joyce appeared unimpressed. 'Perhaps,' she muttered. She looked at Brigitte. 'She went on a bit, didn't she?'

Brigitte nodded. 'Very horsey lady,' she agreed, then quickly pressed a finger to her lips as Penelope reappeared.

As the others made their way upstairs, Ally took Brigitte to one side.

'Apparently Jodi's husband is on his way and will be clearing out her effects,' Ally said, 'so the room will be free when he has done so. Unless, of course, the husband wants to move in.'

Brigitte nodded. 'George will be happy to pay anything extra, I am sure.'

At seven o'clock in the evening, the women walked down to the Craigmonie for dinner. The sun was still shining, the earlier breeze had abated and Ally was pondering whether or not to do an hour's gardening when Jodi's husband arrived.

He was, in a word, shaggy. He had shaggy, shoulder-length greying hair, a long shaggy beard, and even his eyebrows were shaggy. He looked to be about seventy, and he was wielding a large canvas bag.

'Mrs McKinley?'

'Yes,' Ally replied.

'Owen Jones,' he said, by way of introduction, in a strong Welsh accent. 'Jodi's husband. I've come for her things.'

'Oh, Mr Jones, I am so, so sorry about your wife...'

'Yes, well.' He didn't look particularly distressed. 'We've been apart for years.'

'Do come in,' Ally said. 'I'll get the key and show you up to her room.'

'Thank you.' He stepped into the hallway and looked around.

Ally darted into the kitchen to fetch the key, and then closed the door to the hall so that Flora was shut in. She joined him a moment later, indicating that he should follow her up the stairs.

'How did you get here?' she asked.

'I've had to come in my camper van, all the way from Wales to this godforsaken place!' he said, looking morosely out of the window. The view was spectacular from the windows in this room, with its panorama of the village, the river and even the sea loch in the distance, but Locharran's charms were plainly lost on him.

Ally bridled. She didn't like the village being referred to in that way, and, so far anyway, she didn't much like him either.

As she ushered him into the bedroom, she said, 'This must be very distressing for you, and you will let me know if I can help in any way?'

He looked round the bedroom, sniffed loudly and said, 'Don't worry – I'll manage.'

Ally took this as her cue to disappear. 'OK, I'll leave you to it. I'll make some tea – or would you prefer coffee?'

'I won't be hanging around,' he said as he opened the wardrobe door, grabbed a handful of clothes, still on their hangers, and shoved them into the canvas bag.

Ally, feeling deflated, left him to it.

The grieving widower he was *not*. And he was borderline rude. At least he wasn't going to need accommodation if he had a camper van. She peered out of the window to see the vehicle in question and saw a rather old model, extremely dirty. Still, he had come all the way from Wales.

She wouldn't have paired him up with Jodi in a million years. She hoped that he wasn't going to ask if he could park his scruffy van in her little car park at the side of the malthouse.

Ten minutes later, she heard him tramping down the stairs, and went out to meet him in the hallway.

'I've got it all,' he said as he marched towards the door. 'Any chance I can park my van out there?' he asked, pointing vaguely at her little car park.

'I'm afraid not,' Ally said firmly. 'These spaces are for my overnight guests. But I can try to make other arrangements for you. I have a friend with some land who may be able to help you.'

'OK, can you do it now?' he asked gruffly.

'Of course,' Ally said, a little put out by his rudeness.

She telephoned Ross.

'What can I do for you, my lovely?' he asked.

'You could do me a huge favour,' Ally said, keeping her voice low.

'I'm intrigued,' he said.

'I've got the murder victim's husband here and he needs somewhere to park his camper van, so could he possibly come to you?' As well as several upmarket holiday lets, Ross also had some acres of land down by the sea loch.

'No problem,' Ross said. 'Just send him along.'

'You're a treasure – thank you so much.' Ally quickly scribbled down the directions to get to Ross's and handed it to Owen Jones.

Ally followed him out. 'My condolences, Mr Jones,' she said.

He walked down the path to where he'd parked his van, then slung the canvas bag into the passenger seat, got into the driving seat and nodded.

'Thanks,' he said and was gone.

Ally let the dog out. 'You wouldn't have liked him, Flora,' she said before going upstairs to take a look at Room 1. It was completely empty.

SEVEN

Ally had been very touched by what Rigby had told Amir. She was also relieved that he seemed to be making some sort of recovery, and wondered if she could manage to visit him while he was in hospital. As she was serving breakfast, she wondered if she could get a midday train from Fort William, have a couple of hours in Glasgow, and then get a late train back? It would be tight but just about manageable. Just as she was mulling this over, the telephone rang.

'It's Amir here,' he said, 'and I just wanted to let you know that Inspector Rigby has been transferred to hospital in Inverness because he's recovering well and wanted to be closer to home. He's asked me to ask you to visit him as soon as possible. He's in Ward 8.'

That solved the problem. Ally knew she could comfortably drive to Inverness for a hospital visit and be back again a few hours later because it was Magda's, the earl's wife's, birthday today and they'd arranged a dinner at The Bistro in the evening. She decided to ring Rigby there and then, to find out what he could possibly want to talk to her about. It obviously wasn't a matter that could be delayed, and so she dialled the number of the hospital in Inverness.

'My name is Alison McKinley and I've been asked to contact Detective Inspector Rigby, who asked for me to get in touch with him urgently. Would it be possible to visit him this afternoon?'

'I'll put you through to the ward,' the operator said.

The sister on the ward answered the phone, asked her to wait while she checked with Rigby and came back to say, 'The inspector would be very glad to see you as soon as you can get here. He says it's important.'

The journey never failed to impress her, Ally thought as she drove through the mountains, glens and past the little lochs before finally arriving in Fort Augustus and then driving the rest of the way along the side of Loch Ness. The famous loch could be turbulent and quite menacing at times, but today it was calm and deceptively inviting. People had drowned in this loch when its mood had suddenly changed while they were out there in the middle, and their bodies were not always recovered. Whether there was a monster or not, Loch Ness always attracted the tourists, and today was no exception as Ally saw several buses pulled in by the lochside and clusters of people milling around and taking photographs.

Propped up on pillows, Rigby was looking a great deal better than he had when Ally had seen him last. He looked very pleased to see her.

'They've got me stabilised now,' he said, 'and I'm hoping they'll let me home in a day or two – with a mountain of medication, of course.'

'I'm so pleased,' Ally said.

'I want to thank you for what you did when I collapsed at the Craigmonie,' Rigby continued. 'I'm told it was you who stopped the helicopter from leaving until I was taken on board, and that probably saved my life.'

'Well, I'm glad I did,' Ally said, feeling a little emotional.

'Detective Inspector Kandahar will be taking over in the meantime,' he said, 'and I'm sure you'll get on well with him.'

'We've already met,' Ally said, 'and I thought he was charming.'

'He's a good bloke,' Rigby confirmed, 'but he's had a bad time recently. His wife died a couple of years ago and he struggles to keep an eye on his two teenage daughters. So I thought that, as you were such a help to me on my first cases up here, perhaps you'd take him under your wing for a bit? Familiarise him with who's who?'

Take him under my wing for a bit! Ally was immensely flattered that Rigby would suggest such a thing. And it was making her feel quite tearful for both Rigby and Amir Kandahar.

'I really hope you'll be back soon though,' she said truthfully.

He smiled. 'We've had a few arguments, but I want you to know that I've always appreciated your thoughts. And we always got there in the end.'

'We did,' Ally agreed, giving her eyes a wipe. 'And I hope we will again in the future.'

'All thanks to you for getting me on that helicopter!' he said. He paused for a moment then added, 'We've always been so formal, but I wonder if I may call you Ally now? And please call me Bob.'

'Of course you can, Bob,' Ally replied.

'I really appreciate you coming,' Rigby continued, 'because I know you're very busy, but this could be important. Are you here on your own?'

Ally nodded. 'Yes, I am.'

Rigby gazed out of the window for a moment, then cleared his throat. 'This Jodi Jones,' he said, 'the woman who got strangled?'

Ally nodded again.

'I think there's a very good chance she could be my sister,' said Rigby.

Ally could scarcely believe what she was hearing. '*What?*'

'I got a massive shock when I saw her body, which I think triggered this.' He patted his heart.

Ally was confused. 'Your *sister*? Surely you'd have known for certain?'

'I haven't seen her for nearly fifty years,' said Rigby sadly. 'When she was sixteen, my sister left home and vanished. Vanished completely. She was never heard of again. I was only five or six at the time, but it broke my mother's heart. She went to her grave not knowing. In fact, it's one of the reasons I wanted to join the police, become a detective, but of course I never did come across anyone who could be her – until now.'

'Oh, Bob, how awful! Your poor mother! But what on earth makes you think she might be your sister?'

'Several things. She's the spitting image of my mother and...' He paused for a moment. 'The thing that convinced me was the birthmark. She had a birthmark on her neck.'

'Yes, I saw it.' Ally hesitated. 'I saw it when I loosened her scarf.'

'She was always very self-conscious about it, and she nearly always wore high-necked sweaters or scarves to hide it. I was only very little, but the scarves were one of the things I remember about her. I think I could only have seen her birth-mark once or twice. But it fascinated me. The reason I remember it quite clearly is because I thought it was shaped like a goldfish!' He gazed into space again. 'You see, I'd been to the fair and won a goldfish, and I took him home, put him in a bowl and called him Cedric.'

'*Cedric?*' Ally smiled.

'Don't ask me why! I'd seen or heard the name somewhere and obviously fancied it. And I remember thinking that Joanne's strawberry birthmark was very similar in shape to Cedric. It could have been construed as a goldfish, I suppose, bearing in mind how young I was at the time.'

'Do you have any idea why she might have left home?' Ally asked, intrigued.

'Not then, because I was so young, but now I think she'd most probably got herself pregnant. And my mother had always said stuff like, "If a daughter of mine ever got herself pregnant out of wedlock, she needn't ever bother coming back *here!*" My sister's name was Joanne, but she obviously changed that.' He leaned forward. 'I want you to try to find out, Ally. Maybe she has a husband, a child, someone who may now appear out of the blue, and who might be able to tell you something about her.' He lay back and smiled. 'I know you've become something of a super sleuth.'

Ally smiled. 'I've already met your brother-in-law. Jodi's husband turned up to collect her things last night,' she said.

Rigby looked somewhat taken aback. 'So, I have a brother-in-law, do I? What's he like?'

'He's a scruffy, rather unpleasant man by the name of Owen Jones, who she left years ago, but he's still legally her husband I believe. He went up to her room, picked up her things and squashed them all into a big canvas bag, showing no emotion whatsoever.'

Rigby sighed. 'Do you know anything else about Joanne?'

'Well, I've enjoyed her books and, from what I've read, so have lots of other people. She was quite well known in popular fiction circles.' Ally didn't think it was a good idea to tell Rigby about Jodi's torrid love life, not in his current condition. Then she remembered Desdemona's reaction. 'Desdemona Morton said she'd been at university with her.'

'University?' Rigby looked surprised. 'I remember she was clever, but university? How the hell would she have got there without any money?'

'I think I need to talk to Desdemona again and see if I can find out. I had no idea at the time of our conversation that it was going to be of major importance,' Ally said.

'Is this Jones fellow still in the area?'

'He's got a camper van and wanted to leave it in my little car park, but I refused, so he's camped down somewhere on Ross's land. As far as I know he's still there. Have you told Amir Kandahar about Jodi possibly being your sister?'

He shook his head. 'I don't want to at the moment, although I may later, depending on what happens. The thing is, Ally, if my suspicions about Jodi Jones became known, they'd take me off the case because, obviously, I'd be emotionally involved. I don't want to be taken off this case because I'm damned determined to find out who throttled my sister. I just cannot believe that I've gone all these years wondering about her, and then I find this lifeless body...' He wiped his eyes. 'See what you can find out, Ally.'

She patted his hand. 'Don't you worry – I will.'

Privately, she doubted that Rigby would ever be back on this case, but she knew that he mustn't lose hope.

All the way back to Locharran, Ally pondered over what Rigby had said. When she sat down with Ross that evening, she was eager to share her thoughts with him. She told him about Rigby's sister disappearing and how no one had ever discovered what had happened to the sixteen-year-old Joanne Rigby. And that Rigby had asked Ally to discover all she could about Joanne when she first left home.

'How can you possibly find out?' Ross asked.

'Well, I can start by talking to Desdemona,' Ally said, 'and maybe Penelope, because she was at university at the same time.'

'What difference would it make now that the woman's no longer able to meet him?'

Ally sighed. 'He just needs to *know*, Ross. The only member of her family who's appeared so far is the scruffy husband, and he wasn't saying much. Mind you, Jodi had left him years ago, apparently, but never bothered to get a divorce. I feel sorry for Bob Rigby. What a shock he must have got when he saw her body.'

'My suggestion would be that he requests a DNA test or something,' Ross suggested.

'Maybe he'll be able to do that when, and if, he returns to work,' Ally said, 'but he doesn't want his suspicions to become public knowledge. He hasn't told Kandahar or anyone.'

'Well, you don't have time to do anything about it now. We're meeting Hamish and Magda in an hour, so it's time you got ready. Try to put it out of your mind while we entertain Magda tonight,' Ross said with a smile. 'After all, it is her birthday!'

That evening, her head was still full of Rigby's revelations as she got ready for Magda's birthday dinner. Yes, of course she wanted to find out who had killed Jodi, but she also wanted to find out everything she could about the woman, if only to give poor Rigby some closure. She was so preoccupied that she found it difficult to decide what to wear. Finally, she settled on some tailored navy-blue trousers and an emerald-green silk top, which coordinated well. When she looked in the mirror, the colours of Jodi's beautiful scarf came into her mind. She removed the top, hastily placed it back in the wardrobe and chose a cream cashmere sweater instead.

EIGHT

Magda and her husband, the Earl of Locharran – otherwise known as Hamish Sinclair – resided in the hilltop turreted castle above Ally's malthouse. Hamish, who owned almost everything in sight, including the village, was a tall, handsome septuagenarian with more than a passing resemblance to Sean Connery. He had always longed for an heir, but that had never happened in either of his previous marriages, both of which had been unfortunately brief. But it seemed to be third time lucky for him, and after many years as a bachelor, he now had a young wife who was heavily pregnant with twin boys, much to the delight of them both. He and Magda seemed to be blissfully happy, and their heirs were soon to be born, much to the excitement of the village. It was a little like the elusive buses – Hamish having longed for a legal heir for so many years and now there were two coming along at once!

Ally was none too sure that Hamish was aware of all the aspects of fatherhood, such as the prospect of sleepless nights and so forth. Magda had flatly refused to hire any kind of nurse or nanny because she herself was hands-on when it came to babies, having once been a nanny to children whose parents lived all over the globe.

It would be Magda's thirty-fifth birthday, and Ally was very fond of her. Not only that, Ally had had many elaborate meals up in the castle, with or without Ross, and she now felt the need to reciprocate. Since the malthouse was full of murder suspects coming and going, it didn't seem like the ideal location for a celebratory meal, and Ally had had the brilliant idea of booking The Bistro for the occasion, which was conveniently located just down the road from the Craigmonie Hotel.

The owner, Linda, was English, had married a builder from Locharran and arrived in the village some fifteen years previously. Unfortunately, Alastair had died a couple of years later, and Linda was left with the choice of returning south or using her considerable culinary talents to open a business. Fortunately, she chose the latter and now The Bistro was a successful little enterprise. Linda also made desserts for the Craigmonie Hotel, and this had led to her burgeoning relationship with Callum Dalrymple, the hotel manager.

'Magda is enormous, and she won't want to travel far,' Ally had explained to Ross when she had suggested the idea. 'And Linda will appreciate our custom.'

'Oh God!' Linda had exclaimed when Ally approached her. 'What do I cook for *them*?'

'Listen,' Ally said, 'they eat ordinary, plain food most of the time. Honestly! Whatever you do will be a welcome change from Mrs Jamieson's menu. She's a good cook but somewhat conventional and not terribly adventurous, so whatever you do will be a treat.'

After Ally had booked the table, she'd phoned Hamish.

'But we were going to invite you up *here*,' he'd protested.

'No, no, give your ladies a rest. I'd normally have you both here at the malthouse, but, with a houseful of suspects, it would be much nicer at The Bistro. Our treat.'

'We would be honoured,' Hamish had replied. 'Thank you very much.'

Ross insisted on driving Hamish and Magda down from the castle to The Bistro so that they could enjoy a drink – not that Magda was drinking anything stronger than Diet Coke at the moment.

Magda was enormous and, on arrival at the restaurant, she struggled to get herself and her bump anywhere near the table. Nevertheless, once she got there, she ate just about everything in sight, including a few leftovers on Hamish's plate, explaining that she was eating for three.

Linda had done them proud with a choice of seafood or vegetable starters, beef or sea bass main course, and a selection of creamy desserts, and insisted on serving them personally, although she did employ a waitress, and explained the contents of each dish as it was served. She finally sat down and joined them for coffee and liqueurs.

'Do tell me about these women you have staying with you, Alison?' Hamish said as he imbibed a generous measure of Drambuie.

'Well,' said Ally, 'I get the impression that none of them were particularly keen on the victim, and, to be honest, I wasn't too struck on her myself.'

'She wasn't nice?' Magda asked as she popped two chocolate mints into her mouth.

'She was rather overimpressed with herself,' Ally said.

'In what way?' Linda asked.

'I got the impression that she thought her writing was up there with Jilly Cooper and Jackie Collins, and, although I've enjoyed her books, she wasn't in their league,' Ally replied. 'And when I sat in on their writing class on the day she was murdered, she *was* accused of plagiarism.'

'Accused by whom?' Hamish asked.

'By an Irish woman called Della Moran, who'd only just joined the group, and who is now, of course, the main suspect.'

'And is she the only suspect?' Linda asked.

Ally considered for a moment. 'No, there are a number of women suspects, although I can't imagine what motives they might have had. Now that I come to think of it, Joyce, one of my ladies, said more or less the same thing as Della. She, too, reckoned Jodi had nicked one of her ideas.'

'Hmm, interesting. Has the husband appeared yet?' Hamish asked.

'Oh yes,' Ally replied, 'yesterday evening. Bit of a hippy and living in his camper van—'

'On *my land*!' interrupted Ross. 'Scruffy bugger,' he added, 'but he's paid the rent and says he'll be staying until the funeral.'

'So she's going to be buried up *here*?' Hamish asked. 'Why? It's not as if she came from this area?' He looked a little affronted, and Ally wondered if he thought he should have been asked for permission.

'He said that Jodi wanted a funeral that made as little impact on the environment as possible, cardboard coffins and all that sort of thing,' Ross replied. 'He's found a natural burial ground up near Brodale somewhere. I had no idea there was one there, but I daresay people like him are into that sort of thing.' He shrugged. 'He seemed keen to talk about it all for some reason.'

Ally shuddered. 'There was definitely something a bit creepy about him.'

'He told me he lives off-grid in the wilds of Wales, is completely self-sufficient and is not particularly thrilled at being up here. He didn't strike me as being the grieving widower,' Ross commented.

'Me neither,' agreed Ally. 'Then again, I believe they parted company years ago.'

'So who else do you have staying with you?' Hamish asked.

'A mousy little Englishwoman and a sexy little French lady,' Ally replied with a grin. 'And a very loud, aristocratic lady called Penelope Fortescue-Something from the Cotswolds.'

'*Penelope!*' Hamish exclaimed. 'Not Penelope Fortescue-Rawlins, perchance?'

'That sounds like her,' Ally said. 'I know it's a bit of a mouthful, and she mentioned that she knew you.'

Hamish leaned forward. 'Penelope had a roaring affair with Lord Arthur Marsh some years back,' he said gleefully, dabbing his lips with a napkin. 'Then her husband, poor old Herbert, died in *very* mysterious circumstances, supposedly from an overdose. Penelope was accused of crushing tablets and putting them in his whisky. She was actually charged with murder but later released, due to lack of evidence. I'd say that Penelope would be perfectly capable of murder though.'

Ally was quite shocked, particularly as Hamish was so cheerful about the whole thing. She couldn't believe that Penelope could have done something like that. If, of course, she *had* done something like that. 'I wonder if I should tell Amir about this?' Ally realised that she'd unintentionally spoken out loud.

'Who's Amir?' Magda asked.

'Ally has fallen head over heels for the new detective,' Ross said, nudging Ally with a grin.

'I have *not!*' Ally protested. 'But he is very nice.'

'Poor old Rigby had a cardiac arrest when he saw the body,' said Ross. 'But at least he's survived.'

Hamish nodded. 'Well, I hope the man makes a full recovery because, if he doesn't come back, he'll be missed.'

'Oh, I'm not so sure!' Ross exclaimed. 'It didn't strike me that he was that brilliant at doing his job.'

'Now you mention it, I think I agree with you. It seems to me that our dear Alison has been doing most of the detective work in the past year or so.'

'Oh, stop it – you're embarrassing me,' Ally said.
But she was already planning her next move: the board.

NINE

The board was actually the back of a still-life painting positioned on the wall behind the kitchen table. The painting was on a large square piece of wood, and featured an attractive mix of oranges, lemons and grapes, which Ally's grandmother had, many years before, brought back from Italy, presumably from a holiday.

In her previous life as a researcher for a TV company in Edinburgh, Ally had found it very helpful to have a board on the wall on which to stick her findings, and eliminate the ones she no longer wanted or needed, using Post-its. She'd found this method helpful in many ways since, and now, when the painting was removed from the wall and placed face down on the table, the plain wood back provided a good flat surface on which to mount Ally's suspects. To do this it was necessary to tack on a piece of paper, draw a large circle and treat it as a clock, in the middle of which was the victim's name. The chief suspect would then feature at the very top, at twelve o'clock, and the next most likely would be placed at eleven o'clock and one o'clock, whereas the least likely would be at the bottom, at six o'clock. She didn't actually write the numbers down but could visualise them.

So, after Morag had departed the following morning, Ally took the painting down from the wall, turned it over, laid it on the table, and got out the paper and the Post-its. Having drawn the circle – tracing round a dinner plate – and secured it to the board, she then had to think about who her suspects were.

Firstly, she wrote Jodi's name in the centre. Without a doubt, the main suspect had to be Della Moran, so Ally wrote 'Della' on her first Post-it and placed it at the top, at the imaginary twelve o'clock.

Since Hamish's revelations about Penelope, Ally could hardly ignore the possibility of her ability to get rid of someone in her way, but *she'd* invited Jodi along to feature in the writers' retreat so what on earth would be her motive? Unless it was specifically to get the opportunity to murder Jodi? They'd been at university at the same time as each other, so who knew what may have happened between them then, or what hatred or resentment may have lingered?

And what about Joyce? Joyce had admitted openly that she didn't much like Jodi and that Jodi might have stolen one of her ideas too. It made Ally wonder why Joyce had come on the course at all if that was how she felt about Jodi – was it possible that Joyce could have had an ulterior motive? So maybe she should add Joyce to the board, at eleven o'clock perhaps? And pop Penelope on at one o'clock? She had to begin *somewhere*.

Then there was Brigitte. Why had Brigitte been poking around in Jodi's room? Was she just checking it out for her husband's arrival, or was she specifically looking for that diary? Had she torn out that page of the diary which noted her meeting with Jodi, and, if so, why? And what could the meeting possibly have been about that Brigitte felt the need to destroy any evidence of it? Brigitte was certainly a suspect, so perhaps she should be placed at three o'clock? Or should she be placed nearer the top? No, she'd put her at three o'clock, though she'd need to study her closely.

The beauty of this method was that she could then hang the painting back up on the wall and no one – especially her suspects – would know what lurked on the back!

However, there were seven suspects in all, all of whom admitted to visiting the ladies' room in the period before Jodi's death, and she really had to get to know them better if she was going to be any help at all to Detective Inspector Amir Kandahar.

The opportunity came when her four guests got back that evening. Brigitte was very excited because her husband was due to arrive the next afternoon.

It was Penelope, as usual, who, when they all congregated in the hall, said to Ally, 'We have all been having a chat and we've decided to go ahead with our writing until Saturday, as planned. Not that we'd probably be able to leave anyway since we're all under suspicion,' she added. 'We'll need to find out about that. But,' she continued, 'we hear that the funeral is likely to be around here somewhere, and I think, out of respect, we should attend that.'

'We've all paid good money for this week,' Joyce put in, 'so why should we waste a couple of days?'

'And so we wondered if you'd like to come down and give us a little talk tomorrow afternoon?' said Millie.

'*Me?*' Ally was astounded. 'I don't know anything about writing!'

'Perhaps not, but you must have had some interesting experiences in your life,' Penelope said firmly, 'which could give us inspiration for our stories.'

'But I'm not at all interesting...' Ally began.

'Yes, you *are!*' Penelope boomed. 'You left Edinburgh to

come up here to open a guest house, and you weren't in your first flush of youth, were you?'

'No, but—'

'No buts!' ordered Joyce. 'Just a chat about how you came here and what you had to do to get this place up and running.'

'Maybe I should wait here tomorrow until after my husband will arrive,' Brigitte said.

'Just phone him and tell him to come to the Craigmonie,' Millie suggested.

'But—' Brigitte began, interrupted by a forceful Penelope.

'That's settled then,' Penelope roared. 'You'll give us a little talk tomorrow afternoon, Ally. Three o'clock in the Garden Room at the Craigmonie!'

No one argued.

'What did you talk about today?' Ally asked as they all fussed Flora, who had come bounding out of the kitchen.

'It was Joyce's turn today,' Brigitte said, 'and ask us what we don't know about *libraries*!'

'Libraries?' Ally asked.

'Yes, I was a librarian,' Joyce said, 'right up until I retired a couple of years back.' She paused. 'Graham and I never had children, you see, so I always worked.'

'You must be an expert on books then,' Ally remarked.

'She was chief librarian,' Penelope added in her usual loud fashion, 'so she knows a good book when she sees it!'

'Did the job make you think that you could perhaps write too?' Ally asked, turning to Joyce.

Joyce nodded. 'I'd always written essays and things, and then I began to write short stories, mainly about pioneering women and older women. I only sent some to Jodi for editorial advice, and I *still* say she copied a couple of my ideas. It's interesting that I was not the only one. Anyway, I'm exhausted and ready for bed.'

There were general murmurs of agreement, and the women headed upstairs.

And so Ally found herself standing in front of the group of twelve women at three o'clock the next afternoon. It wasn't as scary as she'd thought because they were all really friendly and asked lots of questions, which made it very informal.

They were particularly interested to know about Ally's life as a TV researcher.

'I had to keep finding out about stuff, and it had to be accurate, of course. One minute it might be to get the background of some celebrity or politician who was about to be interviewed, which could be pretty boring unless you came across some naughty incidents! Then, if it was a costume drama, say, I'd have to help the wardrobe department research the clothing, or help the props department on the interiors. Every day was different, and I loved it. The trouble is,' Ally admitted, 'it's made me very nosy!'

There followed the usual questions:

'Did you get to meet lots of famous people?'

'Did you get to travel?'

'Oh yes, I met a few – mainly politicians – and, before we relied on the internet for everything, I did have to travel occasionally. Usually to London but once to Avignon, in the South of France, and once to Milan.' Ally thought fondly of her long-past trips.

'What made you want to buy The Auld Malthouse?' they asked.

'It was just an old storehouse for the malt they made the whisky from, unused and unloved, and no one else seemed interested in buying it,' Ally replied.

'When did you first see it?'

'When I was on holiday.'

'How did your family react?'

'Well,' said Ally, 'they thought I'd gone completely bonkers! I was sixty-six then, and it took a couple of years to buy it and convert the building and so, not unreasonably I suppose, they thought that at that age I should be sitting in my senior's apartment knitting and doing crosswords!' Ally went on to tell them about the village in general, about some of the characters, their attitude to incomers and their love of gossip.

'And you met a *man!*' prompted Joyce.

Ally could feel herself blushing. 'I had a puppy, you see, and I had to take her to the vet for her jabs, and *he* was on duty. I'd expected to see his son, who is the official vet round here, but he was delivering a calf or something and so his father was dragged out of retirement to stand in for him.' Ally paused, then added truthfully, 'Lucky for me!'

'Wow!' exclaimed Della. 'New home! New life! New man!'

'Something like that,' Ally agreed.

'There's going to be a mass immigration of single women up to Locharran now!' joked Millie.

Just then, the tea trolley arrived and everyone rushed to help themselves to refreshments. Standing a little to the side of the group and balancing a cup and saucer in one hand, Ally found herself next to the woman from Cornwall.

'Morwenna, isn't it?' she asked.

Morwenna nodded. 'That's me. Morwenna Davies.'

'Such a lovely Cornish name,' Ally remarked.

'I'm actually Welsh,' the woman said, 'but my mother had become obsessed with Winston Graham's *Poldark* books about Cornwall, and so I had to be named Morwenna. And I actually moved to Cornwall in my twenties because of an unfortunate incident.' She glanced around and lowered her voice. 'I knew Jodi Jones because she had an affair with my husband.' She spoke quite matter-of-factly.

Ally felt her jaw drop. '*She had an affair with your husband?*'

'Yes, not that she particularly wanted him on a permanent basis, of course, but that was what Jodi did. Always trying to be the femme fatale. Tom was weak and stupid, but of course he came crawling back when she eventually spat him out. And do you know what?'

Wide-eyed, Ally shook her head.

'I didn't want the bugger either! So we divorced and I took myself and my daughter down to Penzance, where we'd spent many happy holidays. I've remarried and we've lived there for thirty-five years. And we love it!' She paused. 'Have you tried these biscuits? The ones with the chocolate on them? They are *so* yummy!' With that, she picked one up, dunked it into her tea and popped it into her mouth a split second before it disintegrated.

'Wow!' Ally exclaimed. 'I suppose it's fair to say that you didn't like Jodi much?'

'*Hated* her at the time,' Morwenna agreed cheerfully. 'But I don't hold a grudge against her now because, let's face it, she did me a favour in the long run, and I have another husband now. Still, I think it's for sure that she's upset somebody badly round here, don't you?'

Ally nodded as she gulped her tea and wondered exactly why Morwenna had come on this course.

'In case you're wondering why I'm here,' Morwenna continued blithely as if she'd read Ally's mind, 'I came on this course partly out of pure curiosity. I wanted to see what she looked like now. And I suppose I must have given her a bit of a shock because she didn't know my new surname, and so she wouldn't have known it was me until I got here.'

'I'm coming to the conclusion that Jodi was less than popular generally,' Ally admitted, wondering just how crowded her suspect board was going to become. Was Morwenna *really* not bothered by something that had happened so many years before? Surely her pride would have been dented a little? She would require adding to the board, probably at four or five o'clock.

Morwenna was now chatting with Anne, the retired nurse, and Ally turned her attention to the rather drab woman sitting on her other side. She had long, straight hair, pale skin and a permanent frown. She was certain that this was the seventh woman who'd admitted to visiting the ladies' room.

'I'm Laura,' she said, confirming Ally's suspicions. 'I think I'm a suspect cos I left this room during that coffee break.'

'I bet you wish you hadn't,' Ally remarked with a smile.

'Bloody right!' said Laura, draining her cup and waving at one of the other women who was standing by the trolley. 'I'm going up for a refill.' With that, she stood up, headed towards the tea trolley and began chatting to her friend.

Ally was none the wiser whether Laura had any history with Jodi, but then there hadn't been much time for her to be particularly forthcoming. Ally made a mental note to try to find an opportunity to talk to her again.

She looked around and decided that this was as good a time as any to make her escape when Della Moran appeared at her side.

'I enjoyed your talk,' she said politely.

'Well, thank you,' Ally replied. 'I had nothing prepared because they only asked me last night. How are you?'

Della shook her head. 'Women can be very bitchy,' she said.

'They all seem so nice individually,' Ally remarked with a sigh. Except Laura, she thought, who was bordering on rude.

'They're all trying to save their own skins,' Della continued, 'which is why they're giving me a hard time. But, believe me, I'm not the only one whose stories she pinched! And I really wish I was staying up at your malthouse because they're all gunning for me here.'

Ally thought for a moment. 'Brigitte's husband is due to arrive today and she's moved into what was Jodi's room, which is a double. Penelope's now on her own in a twin-bedded room so I suppose you could always move in with her.'

Della rolled her eyes heavenward. 'She's so fecking *loud!*'

'I'm told she snores loudly too,' Ally added with a grin.

'I think I'll stay right here then,' Della said.

Della was a very attractive woman with her shoulder-length red hair and very blue eyes, which was a quite unusual combination. Ally estimated that she was in her fifties and wondered how, from somewhere near Belfast, she had become involved with Jodi.

'The thing is,' Della went on, 'Jodi Jones was supposedly a reputable editor as well as a successful writer. She advertised her editing and proofreading skills in the writing magazines and online. She had her own website. And she charged a bloody fortune to look through your manuscript. "Let me sort out your books and I can almost guarantee publication" she spouted. So people did. And I'll bet that half of the women in this room probably did.'

'Was she a good editor?' Ally asked.

'Yes, she was. She was excellent, and she was considered to be worth the money. But that's not *all* she did!'

'Really?'

'Oh no!' Della leaned forward and placed her hand on Ally's arm. 'Like I said, she pinched all her ideas from other people's stories.'

'Do you really think so?' Ally asked.

'I bloody well *know* so!' Della exclaimed loudly. Then, lowering her voice: 'She'd return your manuscript, highlighting all the things she considered to be wrong, but she'd be saving your ideas, your plots, and use them later on as one of her own. That is what she *did!*'

'Surely, as a well-established writer, she had plenty of ideas of her own?' Ally suggested.

'She did well with her first book, bestseller, blockbuster, and all that, and so she thought she could do no wrong. But she was short of ideas so she'd wait a respectable amount of time, and then out would come the next book when she'd stolen someone else's plot. Time and time again!' Della looked around. 'I came up here on her so-called writing retreat to confront her, and I don't think I'm the only one. I just happened to be the first to open my mouth.'

Ally thought for a moment. 'So why did the others not agree with you when you accused Jodi? Why are they pointing a finger at you?'

'Because I am the scapegoat,' Della replied. 'They all want to divert the blame away from themselves. I bet that even the half-dozen women who *didn't* go to the loo were pipped to the post. Someone was very, very clever!' Della narrowed her eyes, nodded in agreement with herself and headed off towards the biscuits.

Ally's thoughts were beginning to crystallise. What if Della was right? Perhaps *all* the women had come north with the intention of killing Jodi Jones, but only seven had had the opportunity!

Perhaps Joyce really *had* had her idea stolen. Perhaps Penelope was quite capable of murder. Perhaps Morwenna still bore a grudge about her husband's affair with Jodi. But what about Millie and Brigitte? What was it with Brigitte and that diary? And the enigmatic Laura? Could they *all* have had their ideas and plots stolen by Jodi Jones?

When Ally got home, she realised that she only had one further suspect for the moment: Morwenna, although she did seem a little unlikely. She sat down with coffee and the board, wrote 'Morwenna' on a Post-it and positioned it at five o'clock, although she wasn't entirely sure why. She was aware that she wasn't making much progress so far.

She sighed, hung the painting back on the wall and began to prepare some supper for Ross when he came up later. She then wondered if Brigitte's husband had showed up.

Brigitte's husband, who was called George, had arrived in the afternoon as planned, but Ally didn't set eyes on him until the following morning when George appeared with Brigitte at breakfast time. He was English, short and stocky, good-looking and had dark hair and a trendy little beard. He also seemed to be considerably older than Brigitte, and he reminded Ally of someone, but she couldn't think for the life of her who it was. They both looked rather pleased with themselves, so Ally assumed they'd had a good night in what had briefly been Jodi's bed. He seemed pleasant enough and, like most men, ate everything on offer.

Ally had set up two tables, one for Brigitte and George, and one for the other three. Most of the women settled for a simple continental breakfast, although Penelope wanted 'the lot'.

The women had now organised some sort of schedule that enabled them to have writing and critiquing classes, morning and afternoon, determined to do something constructive while they were booked in at the Craigmonie. It meant that they left the malthouse at half past nine to begin their first session at ten or ten thirty. This also meant that the rooms were vacated quite early and Morag was able to get their cleaning done without interruption.

Ally was curious about George as Brigitte had given her no indication as to what he might be doing all day. But after they'd finished eating, George approached Ally and complimented her on the breakfast. Then he added, 'In case you were wondering, I shall be joining the ladies today, while I'm here, down at the Craigmonie Hotel.'

'Do you write too?' Ally asked.

'No, I'm a publisher, small time, and mainly textbooks, dictionaries, educational – not at all the sort of thing these ladies write! But I'm happy to help with the critique, and I shall take my laptop with me so I can continue working – if I can find a quiet corner.' He hesitated. 'I know we're only booked until tomorrow, but I wondered if we might stay on for another week, because it is very beautiful here and neither of us have been this far north before?'

'I've no further bookings for that room for a few weeks yet,' Ally replied, 'so I'd be very happy to have you stay on for another week.'

After they'd gone, Ally wondered about the significance of this. Perhaps Brigitte knew a thing or two about Jodi, via the publishing world? It did seem highly unlikely though that Jodi would be having textbooks or dictionaries printed. Nevertheless, rumours would undoubtedly circulate in the publishing world, true or otherwise, and Ally couldn't help but wonder if there were more secrets in Jodi's past that might be uncovered?

TEN

After Morag had cleaned the bedrooms, had her mug of tea and gone home, Ally decided to take her still-life down from the wall and maybe move Brigitte to six o'clock. But, just then, she heard the doorbell, and hastily hung the board up again. She had a visitor: Amir Kandahar.

'Good morning, Ally,' he said. 'I hope I haven't come at an inconvenient time?'

'Not at all,' Ally replied. 'Do come in. Do you mind if we go into the kitchen?'

'Certainly not,' he said. 'I'm very fond of kitchens. And this,' he added as she led him inside, 'is a particularly nice one.'

'Rigby liked a cup of tea and shortbread,' Ally told him.

'Let me carry on the tradition,' said Amir, 'but no milk in my tea, please. And one spoonful of sugar.'

'That's exactly how I take it.' Ally was now feeling more than ever that here was a kindred spirit, particularly as he made a great fuss of Flora. As she handed him his tea, she asked, 'Have you any news?'

He shook his head. 'Unfortunately, not a great deal. I've interviewed all the women at the retreat now and believe that we can discount those who didn't leave the room in the period in question. I've also interviewed the Craigmonie staff who were on duty and the few guests who were in the hotel at that time, none of whom were anywhere near the writers' retreat section, apart from one or two people in the bar, and they were in full view of the bar staff the whole time. That now leaves the seven possibilities: the four who are staying here – Joyce Williams, Penelope Fortescue-Rawlins, Brigitte Atkins and Millie Day – plus the three ladies at the Craigmonie: Della Moran, Laura Pike and Morwenna Davies.'

'Did you know that one of them, Brigitte Atkins, has now been joined by her husband who is a publisher of educational books?'

'That would exclude him publishing most of these women's books then, from what I gather,' Amir added with a smile. 'The French lady did in fact inform me of this, and I've checked with the company who have confirmed that they concentrate on text-books, dictionaries and educational stuff, and I gather that Miss Jones's work did not quite fit in to any of these categories.'

'Hardly!' Ally confirmed with a grin.

'However, since all of these women are writers, or aspiring writers, I cannot rule any of them out because of their possible connection, however slim, with the publishing world.' He shuf-fled some papers. 'I understand that Miss Jones was accused of plagiarism by a couple of the suspects?'

'Oh yes,' Ally said, 'and they've been completely honest about it, particularly Della Moran.'

Amir nodded. 'Interesting character, that. I really just wanted to remind you that one of your guests could well be the killer, and so, if you see or hear anything about them that might be relevant, I'd be grateful if you could let me know.' He looked at Ally a little anxiously. 'I'm not suggesting you snoop or anything...'

'I get what you're saying,' Ally said, and then a thought

struck her. 'I had a chat with the earl the other evening and he knew Penelope Fortescue-Rawlins from years ago. She's a bit of an aristocrat too, you know.'

He frowned and shuffled his papers some more. 'She's the woman who speaks very loudly?'

'That's her,' Ally confirmed. 'And Hamish – the earl – said that she was once suspected of killing her husband.'

Amir stopped shuffling and looked at Ally long and hard. 'What?'

'Apparently, she'd been having an affair with Lord Somebody-or-other, and her husband supposedly took his own life, but there was some suggestion that he'd been murdered. She was actually arrested but later released, due to lack of evidence. However, the earl seemed to think that she would be quite capable of murder.'

'Hmm,' said Amir. 'I may have to speak to the earl, but I haven't met him yet. Is he a nice man?'

'He's a charming man,' Ally replied.

'His information would be reliable?'

'Without a doubt.'

Amir took out his phone. 'Remind me where this woman lives?'

'In the Cotswolds, somewhere in Gloucestershire, I believe. But I do have all their addresses in my visitors' book if you need them.'

Amir smiled in thanks. 'I do have a list of their addresses, and now I will be contacting their local police departments.' He drained his cup and stood up.

'Where are you based?' Ally asked.

'Well, Glasgow really, but temporarily with the Inverness police. I believe Detective Inspector Rigby had a bungalow or something converted into a temporary police station while he was here?'

Ally nodded. 'He did.'

'Depending on how long this case goes on for, I might find it helpful to continue using that, so I'll look into it.' He handed her a card. 'Please get in touch if you should discover anything at all that might be relevant.'

'I will,' Ally promised. 'I honestly don't know if this is important or not, but Brigitte Atkins was extremely keen to occupy Room One, mainly because her husband was about to join her. But when I went upstairs a few days ago, before he arrived, I found Brigitte in there, looking at Jodi's diary, and after she left I looked at the diary and noticed that a page – this week's page – had been torn out, but I could decipher, from the indented section on the previous page, something about her having a chat with Brigitte.' Ally opened a drawer. 'I do have the diary here. It had fallen down the back of the chest of drawers so Owen Jones didn't see it when he came for Jodi's things, but I thought it could be relevant.' She handed it to him.

Amir examined the diary. 'Rigby was right – you really are quite a sleuth.'

Ally felt ridiculously pleased.

'Perhaps Jodi Jones knew her from before?' Amir suggested.

'Possibly. I just wondered.'

'I'll have a word with her. You will let me know if any similar incident occurs?'

'Yes, of course,' Ally replied, glancing guiltily at her still-life on the wall. *I wonder what he'd think of that*, she mused, *if he turned it over?* She accompanied him to the door and waved him off.

After he'd gone, she realised that she should have asked him if the women would be allowed to leave when the week was up. And, if they weren't, who'd be paying?

Callum Dalrymple arrived on the malthouse doorstep just before midday, settled himself in the sunny kitchen next to the biscuit tin and, fixing his Paul-Newman-type blue eyes on Ally, said, 'One of these damned women, Ally, is the killer – has to be, so let's just hope that this Kandahar fellow is more clued up than Rigby was.'

'Rigby wasn't so bad,' Ally murmured in his defence, handing him a mug of coffee.

Callum ignored her remark. 'Now,' he said, 'the five women who did not visit the ladies' room that afternoon have been excluded as suspects and are all leaving tomorrow, as originally planned. And I must emphasise that none of my other guests were anywhere near there at the time. Most were out for the day, and the couple who remained were sitting down by the river. There was a man chatting up Miss Jones at the bar, and we're trying to locate him.' He paused for a moment. 'I can't for the life of me think why anyone would want to kill the woman! I mean, so what if she did steal the Irishwoman's story? Is that worth a life sentence?'

'Unlikely,' Ally agreed. 'I'm coming to the conclusion that there's more to it than that. Possibly something connected with their personal lives?'

'Maybe.' Callum shook his head. 'Anyway, what I came to tell you is that Laura and Morwenna want to stay on at the Craigmonie for another week, but they want a room each and they're happy to pay. Della can't make up her mind at the moment but has promised to let me know by tomorrow.'

'I've no idea what my lot plan to do,' Ally said, 'except for Brigitte. Her husband has arrived, and they want to stay on, as tourists, for another week too.'

Callum nodded. 'Good. I understand that all seven of them have been told by the police that they are free to go home but that their local police stations would be alerted to the fact that they are murder suspects, so they'd have to check in there once a week and hand in their passports, just in case they decided to abscond.'

'I don't suppose they'd like that,' Ally said.

'What will the neighbours think?' Callum joked in a falsetto voice. He grinned. 'So don't be surprised if your women decide to stay on.'

Ross was working in the surgery all that afternoon, and Ally decided to drive Flora and herself down to his house, to take Flora and Ebony for a walk around the grounds. Ally often stayed there overnight in the winter, but when the guests arrived, she obviously had to be at the malthouse.

Ebony was highly delighted to see both her and Flora, and they set off round Ross's domain. Both his cottages were let out, so she gave them a wide berth, and headed towards the river and the loch. It was the same river that flowed through Locharran, the Altbeag, but closer to where it flowed into the sea loch and then into the Atlantic.

It was a beautiful day, and she stopped for a moment to listen to the blackbird singing above in one of the trees, enthralled as always by the deep, throaty, melodic tones. Every year she'd always waited for the blackbirds to commence singing, usually in March, and then she knew that spring had arrived. Sadly, by July he'd stop trying to attract the females and he'd fall silent for another year.

Ally moved towards the river, weaving a path through the wild garlic and avoiding nettles. And then she saw it: Owen Jones's scruffy camper van. She walked slowly in that direction, wondering if he might be around. Perhaps she should ask about the funeral?

As luck would have it, she saw him coming out and crouching over what was plainly a camping stove. He must have heard her coming because he stood up and stared in her direction.

'We meet again!' Ally exclaimed, hoping she sounded hearty enough.

He scowled, as if trying to remember.

'I'm Ally McKinley from The Auld Malthouse,' she reminded him.

He nodded. 'What do you want?'

'I don't *want* anything,' Ally said sharply. 'I just happen to be here walking on my friend's land when I saw your van.' She was conscious of the fact that he kept walking towards her while looking back anxiously at the van. Was he trying to hide something – or somebody? She could have sworn she saw some movement inside the limited space of the camper van.

Keen to stay on for a few minutes longer, Ally asked, 'Have any arrangements been made for Jodi's funeral?'

There was more movement inside the van, and he looked back nervously. What or who was he trying to hide?

'A week on Sunday, in the morning, eleven o'clock,' he said, 'at the natural burial site. I've told the bloody police, so if you need any information, ask them.' With that, he gave her a final glare before tracing his steps back towards the van.

Aware of being 'dismissed', Ally nodded, shouted at the dogs and moved away.

She was quite sure that there had been someone in that van. But who?

When they all arrived back in the evening, it was Joyce who approached Ally.

'Ally,' she asked hesitantly, 'would it be OK if Penelope, Millie and myself stayed on for another week? The police have told us that Jodi is to be buried somewhere around here next Sunday, and we all feel we should go.' She hesitated for a moment and then said, 'She's being buried in a *field*!'

'I think you mean a natural burial ground,' Ally said with a wry smile. 'Yes, of course you can stay. I gather that two of the ladies at the Craigmonie are staying on too. Is that why you've come to this decision?'

'Well,' said Joyce, looking surreptitiously over her shoulder, 'there are several reasons. One is that we all get on well and enjoy each other's company. Another is because we're writers and so we're naturally curious to know who killed poor Jodi, and what a plot that might provide for our next books!' She paused for a moment. 'And, Ally, we all love The Auld Malt-house – and you! Also, we'd like to see more of this part of the world and, because none of us are exactly on the breadline, we are fortunate enough to be able to afford to stay on for the extra week.'

Ally felt quite moved by her comments. 'I'd love you to stay,' she confirmed, wondering how much information she could elicit from the ladies in the week ahead.

When she went back into the kitchen, she made herself a coffee and sat down at the table. Another week. Callum was right, and the women did not appear to be in any hurry to go home for whatever reason. Could it just be because they wanted to stay for Jodi's funeral? Was it because of the neighbours finding out that they were murder suspects? Or that six out of the seven were desperate to know who the killer was? Or was it just to give them ideas for their own plots? She recalled Desdemona's remarks about the real motives for killing: love, hate, jealousy, revenge. Could it be possible that at least one of the women had come to the writing retreat solely to kill Jodi? But who? And why?

Ally had a week to try to help DI Kandahar – and Rigby, of course – on this one. Four of the women were right here, under her roof. She'd try to find time to chat to them individually because they might tell her things that they wouldn't necessarily disclose to a man. She wondered how she could find a way to befriend the three down at the Craigmonie, not that Della had confirmed yet if she was staying or not.

She studied her still-life painting, but there was no point in removing it from the wall until she could narrow down the suspects.

Her thoughts returned to Rigby. Jodi Jones certainly appeared to be his sister, and the poor man needed to find out who had killed her. She felt rather guilty that she had done nothing yet to try to find out more about Jodi's life, as she had promised Rigby she would do. She had every hope that she could do both though – find the killer and the details of Jodi's personal life, which were so important to Bob Rigby.

ELEVEN

It was a beautiful calm, sunny evening, and Ally did what she always did when she needed to be on her own and do some thinking.

'Come on, Flora,' she called. 'Let's have a walk to Loch Soular.'

Flora was doing well with two walks in one day, but she wagged her tail furiously in anticipation. She loved the twenty-minute walk to the little loch, running through the moorland heather and sniffing hopefully at every rabbit hole, and then digging in the muddy sand that surrounded the loch. Ally had learned the hard way, by falling flat on her face in the heather, to avoid the entrances to these rabbit warrens, and now took a stick with her to test the ground ahead. She was delighted to see clumps of fresh green grass pushing up in between the heather. Summer was almost here.

As they approached Loch Soular, Flora began to bark excit-edly, which generally meant that there was someone around. Ally sighed, her thoughts of peaceful contemplation vanishing in the breeze. There was a swimmer in the loch, doing a steady, powerful crawl to the far end, then turning round and swimming all the way back towards where Ally was standing. Whoever it was, they were a strong swimmer and, not only that, Ally thought, the water must still be icy after the long, bitter winter.

'Nice loch,' Millie remarked nonchalantly as she stepped ashore, wiping water from her eyes. Her sturdy body was encased in a plain, black, no-nonsense swimsuit, the kind used by serious swimmers, and her skin was very pink.

'Millie!' Ally exclaimed. 'You are one magnificent swimmer! And that water must be *so* cold!'

Millie rubbed her nose. 'Yeah, well, I like cold-water swimming, and this is no worse than most at this time of year.' She wandered across to where she'd placed a large beach towel behind a boulder, wrapped it round and began to dry herself.

Ally waited until Millie, still wrapped in the towel, settled herself down on the boulder. She might be small and mousy, but, my goodness, couldn't she swim!

'My parents chucked me into the pool as a baby,' Millie said with a grin, 'and I think it's fair to say that I've probably swum most days since. I was on the list for the Barcelona Olympics in 1992, you know, but didn't quite make it.'

'I wish my parents had done that,' Ally remarked ruefully, 'because I was much older when I learned to swim and I've never been really confident in water.' She watched as Millie dug a T-shirt out of a bag. 'I'm pleased that you ladies are staying on for an extra week.'

Millie nodded. 'We all agreed. None of us has anything special to go back for.' She looked intensely at Ally. 'Writing is quite a solitary occupation, and it's nice to mix with other women who feel the same.' She looked around. 'Just look at this scenery! And that magical castle up there! So we came to write, but I think we're staying on as tourists.'

'I couldn't be more delighted,' Ally said truthfully. She

waited for a moment, then said, 'So, there's no one at home to object to your plan?'

Millie was towelling her hair. 'No.'

Ally wondered how to get her to open up a little. 'That's good in a way, isn't it? It means you can do what you like.'

'It does,' Millie agreed.

This was her first chance to try to extract some information from Millie, but she wasn't being particularly forthcoming.

Ally tried again. 'You're not married then?'

'I was.'

'I'm sorry,' Ally said, feeling a little guilty. 'I didn't mean to pry.'

'That's OK,' said Millie but offered no further information.

Ally tried hard to think of something to draw this woman out. 'So, have you enjoyed the course, apart obviously from Jodi's murder?'

Millie patted Flora's head. 'Yes, I've quite enjoyed the week. It's been interesting to say the least.'

'And you're OK sharing a room with Joyce?'

'Joyce is all right. She's been giving me some good advice because she's the only one of us to have four short stories published,' Millie replied.

'And then there's Penelope,' Ally said, wondering if she might be overdoing it.

'God, she's so posh and so *loud*!' Millie exclaimed. '*And bossy!*'

Ally laughed. 'It takes all types.'

'You've got them all here.' Millie looked around. 'Do you think anyone can see me if I get out of this swimsuit and get into my clothes?'

'I don't think they can,' Ally replied, turning around diplomatically and looking in the opposite direction.

Ally and Millie, with Flora romping ahead, walked back to the malthouse together, but Millie wasn't giving away any personal information. They spoke about the scenery, the view, dogs and the weather. Millie wasn't nearly as forthcoming as the others and was plainly a more private person. Somehow or other, Ally was going to need to find a way to befriend her, if possible, and try to discover what made this little woman tick.

Ross had gone home while Ally was doing breakfasts on Sunday morning and came back mid-morning after the women had left.

'I have an interesting snippet of news for you,' he said with a grin as he and Ebony settled themselves in the kitchen.

Ally looked at him expectantly.

'When I took Ebony out for a walk, I saw one of your Craigmonie suspects sneaking out of Owen Jones's camper van!'

'*What? Who?*'

'Can't remember her name. The gloomy-looking one – the one you weren't keen on?'

'What, Laura? Average height, straight brown hair?'

'I'm pretty sure that's her,' Ross confirmed. 'Now, I don't suppose she was visiting to give him writing lessons, particularly as she came out of the van with her clothes over her arm and then finished getting dressed. Not much room in those vans, you know!'

'Laura's been sleeping with Jodi's husband?' Ally murmured slowly, trying to digest this information. 'Oh my God!'

'I thought you'd be interested,' Ross added with a grin.

'That's something that Amir will also be interested in,' Ally said, amazed.

Everything was falling into place now: Laura! Laura, the not-very-friendly one. Laura, who didn't socialise. Of course she didn't socialise – because she was visiting her lover. Owen had been here for almost a week now, and Laura had her own room at the hotel. The other writers, Morwenna and perhaps Della had left, so no one would know if she was in or out.

Ally deduced that Laura must have been Owen's lover for some time, and the only obstacle standing in her way to wedded – or otherwise – bliss, was Jodi, Owen's wife who, perhaps, had some sort of hold over him or refused to divorce him. Perhaps Jodi sent him some of her royalties on condition he remained single? But why would Laura care?

Ally thought again of what Desdemona had said about the prime motives for killing. Jealousy and hatred came to mind, and perhaps Laura qualified on both counts? Had she come on this course purely to kill Jodi, and Owen had then joined her once he knew his wife was dead? Had it been meticulously planned? A set-up job!

Ally removed the board from the wall, turned it over, moved Della and Penelope down an hour and placed Laura at twelve o'clock.

The earl made a surprise visit on Sunday mid-morning.

'Good to see you, Hamish,' Ally greeted him as he sat down in the kitchen, 'and how's Magda?'

Hamish rolled his eyes. 'The poor girl is very uncomfortable because these are big babies. And she doesn't want me anywhere near her! Only a few more weeks to go, thank God.'

He was in for a bit of a shock because, as most women knew, even one baby could, temporarily at least, wreck their routine, and two were impossible to imagine.

'Isn't this weather glorious?' Hamish added, looking out through the window.

The weather was indeed glorious. The clouds had disappeared overnight, the temperature had shot up, and everyone in Locharran has begun to shed their coats and sweaters. Not that they ever trusted the weather to stay that way because, in this part of the world, the temperature could drop by ten or fifteen degrees overnight, for no specific reason, and so these cast-offs could not be packed away for the summer months, as they might be further south. Most highlanders eyed the sky in the morning with mistrust, and then prepared for the worst.

'Yes, it's surprisingly warm for May,' Ally agreed, wondering when she'd ever get time to tidy up her straggling garden.

'What I've really come for,' said Hamish, 'is to find out what's happening with your ladykillers.'

Ally laughed. 'Ladykillers! What a brilliant name.'

'Well, one of them must definitely be a ladykiller, I would assume,' Hamish said.

'They've all decided to stay on for another week,' Ally said, 'with the possible exception of the Irish lady, who hadn't decided when last I spoke to Callum. She's one of the chief suspects too. Anyway, all the others seem to be enjoying it here.'

Ally suddenly had an idea. 'Perhaps you wouldn't mind if I suggested they take a walk up to the castle, just to see it at close quarters? They've all remarked on how magnificent it is.'

'Certainly,' Hamish confirmed. 'In fact, why not bring them up this very afternoon while the sun is shining. Perhaps show them around a bit...' He hesitated momentarily. 'Show them the gardens maybe? I know! Why don't we have a picnic on the lawn above the Italian garden? Do you think they'd like a picnic, Alison?'

'I'm sure they'd love a picnic. But you really don't have to go to these lengths.'

'Yes,' confirmed Hamish, 'that is what we'll do. We'll have a picnic for you, Ross and the ladykillers in the castle gardens at half past three. I've checked the weather and it's set to be fair for the next couple of days.'

'That's very sweet of you,' Ally said, wondering if Magda was aware that he planned to entertain so many ladies on his lawn. 'I have to warn you that there's one husband as well, belonging to the French lady.'

'French, eh?' Hamish looked impressed. 'Apart from anything else, I fancy reacquainting myself with my old friend, Penelope. Friend or not, though, I'm damned sure she's your killer!' He paused. 'Surely these ladies wouldn't have anything better to do on a sunny Sunday afternoon?'

'I'm sure you're right,' Ally agreed. 'Have you time for a cup of tea?'

'No, thank you, my dear. I must be on my way. See you all at three thirty!'

The literary ladies were cock-a-hoop when they got back to the malthouse.

'A real *earl*!' Joyce exclaimed.

'Oh, wow, wait till I tell them this back home!' said Millie.

'Somebody needs to go down to tell Morwenna and Laura,' Joyce said, 'and what about Della? Has she decided yet if she's staying or going?'

'I bet she'll stay when she hears about this,' said Millie.

'It's years since I last saw the old devil!' Penelope boomed. 'Can't believe anyone's married him, given his age and reputation!'

'I think you'll find he's a changed man,' Ally remarked. 'And his wife is only a few weeks away from giving birth to twins.'

Penelope hooted. '*I've* had twins! Both off my hands now, thank God. I shall certainly be able to give her some first-hand advice, like where to find a decent nanny and all that.'

That should be an interesting conversation, Ally thought, since Magda had no intention of employing a nanny.

. . .

Ross had been talking about trying to find somewhere different to eat on a Sunday evening, and so Ally thought it was best to call him before he made any arrangements.

'Hamish is hosting a *picnic?*'

Ally could hear the disbelief in his voice.

'Yes, for all the women, who he calls the Ladykillers! I think he's just curious.'

'Hmm,' said Ross. 'The old bugger probably just wants to be surrounded with ladies all afternoon.'

'Oh, *Ross!*'

'Once a lothario, always a lothario! Not that I think he's going to be wildly excited by any of that lot, with the possible exception of the red-haired Irish lady.'

'Yes, she's very attractive,' Ally agreed.

'Shall I wear my shorts?' Ross asked.

As the remaining ladies had decided to relax over the weekend, they were all free to go to the picnic. After that, Ally assumed they would all do their own thing the following week; time to contemplate, and to write and to enjoy the countryside. That was, after all, what they were supposed to be here for.

The only person who was staying on but not the slightest bit interested in the earl's picnic was Laura. She'd apparently said something to the effect that she'd prefer to watch grass grow than kowtow to some hereditary peer with a brain probably about the size of a peanut. Ally wasn't entirely surprised. Apart from having found Laura somewhat rude and offhand, she was plainly having an affair with Owen. And she was now top of the board!

TWELVE

Everyone walked up to the castle. The Scottish saltire had been erected on the flagpole solely in their honour, although Ally wasn't sure that they were aware of that. The path to the Italian garden wound around the western side of the castle, and on the nearby lawn, a spectacular buffet had been set up on a long table draped in white tablecloths. There was seafood galore, crab, shrimps, prawns, salmon, trout, plus quiches, pies and all manner of salads, plus several bottles of wine chilling in an ice bucket.

The women gasped.

'Good old Hamish!' Ross exclaimed to Ally. 'Trust him to do it in style.'

'I should think poor Mrs Jamieson and Mrs Fraser have been busy for hours,' Ally added.

'My God!' exclaimed Joyce. 'Whatever happened to squashed sandwiches and Thermos flasks of tea?'

'And bottles of lukewarm lemonade,' added Millie, stroking a bottle of chilled white wine. 'This isn't a picnic – it's a banquet.'

Ally laughed. 'They like to do things properly up here.'

As the women oohed and aahed round the table, Hamish made an appearance, looking very jaunty in his white shirt and green tartan kilt.

'Welcome, ladies!' he called. 'Please do help yourselves to whatever you fancy and sit down in the sunshine, while it lasts.'

A couple of the women had brought towels to sit on, but these were made completely redundant because there were little tables and chairs all over the lawn.

'This is so lovely!' Brigitte exclaimed, while her husband headed straight for the wine.

'Well, Hamish,' shouted Penelope. 'Long time no see!'

'Dear girl,' Hamish replied. 'How *are* you?'

'All the better for seeing you, you old goat!' Penelope replied. 'What's all this about you getting married?'

As if on cue, Magda waddled out from the door behind, and Hamish put his arm round her and kissed her fondly. 'This is what's happened to me, Pen. Meet Magda, my lovely wife.' He pointed at Magda's belly. 'My two sons are in there.'

Everyone had stopped staring at the buffet and were now staring at Magda.

Magda smiled and said, 'I hope you won't mind if I don't join you, but I can't really take the heat at this stage in my pregnancy.' She gave a little wave and retreated indoors.

A moment later, Hamish and Penelope were deep in conversation, and the other women surrounded Ally and Ross, remarking on what a handsome old man he was, and how had he managed to get himself such a lovely young wife?

'That's a very long story,' Ally replied, laughing, 'which I'm not prepared to go into. Come on, girls – let's eat.'

Plates were loaded, glasses filled, and everyone sat down at one of the tables to enjoy the food. Ally sat down with the two from the Craigmonie, while Ross regaled the other four with the story of his coming up to Locharran forty years ago from Glasgow, shortly after he'd qualified as a vet.

'My God,' said Morwenna, 'Laura was a fool to miss out on this.'

'Well, she's an oddball,' Della said, shelling a shrimp. She'd finally decided to stay.

'Never joins in much,' added Morwenna. 'Wait until we tell her about today.'

'Don't know what she gets up to,' Della went on. 'Seems to resent everyone and everything. Then again, she's probably convinced herself I'm a killer, so maybe she wants to give me a wide berth.'

Ally studied Della through her sunglasses, convincing herself that – for no good reason whatsoever – she didn't think that Della *was* a killer. But would a jury think that if it came to a trial?

Looking at Morwenna, she couldn't really see her as a killer either. *I'm getting soft,* Ally thought, *because one of these seven has got to be the damned culprit. It's becoming more and more likely it's Laura, isn't it?*

Hamish left Penelope loading up her plate and turned his attention to his other guests, asking them their names and where they came from, laying on the charm. Despite being a happily married man, he was still, predictably, drawn first to Brigitte and, a little later, to Della.

Mrs Fraser, the earl's housekeeper, was now placing bowls of fruit and desserts on the table, and telling everyone that the ice cream was available just inside the door where it was cooler. There followed a further stampede towards the buffet, where some had seconds and others attacked the desserts.

'You've done us proud, Hamish,' Ally said when she finally got him on his own. 'Now, have you decided which one of these ladies could be the killer?'

'Oh,' said Hamish quite matter-of-factly, 'that'll be Penelope. She said she couldn't stand the Jones woman, and neither could the others.' He paused for a moment. 'Which brings me to the obvious question – why did they all come to Locharran?'

'Apart from the fact they were attending a literary retreat, do you mean?' asked Ally.

Hamish stroked his beard. 'Perhaps they *all* came here to kill her, but Penelope beat them to it! Got there first, eh? She's a bloody strong woman, you know. I've watched her roping horses, hunting and all that. I should think she could strangle anyone in a couple of minutes flat!'

Ally could hear the admiration in his voice, which was hardly appropriate if Penelope *was* the killer. And if Penelope was as strong as Hamish made out, then she could most certainly have strangled Jodi.

Everyone lingered on the lawn in the sunshine. After a short time, Hamish asked to be excused, told them all to stay on as long as they liked, said they were welcome to have a look at the Great Hall and thanked them for coming.

'He's thanking *us*!' Brigitte said in amazement. '*What* a gentleman.'

George, her husband, was taking photos of everything in sight. 'I've been to a few chateaux in my time,' he said, eyeing his wife, 'but this is my first experience of a Scottish castle *bathed in sunshine!*'

'A rare sight this early in the year,' Ross agreed, smiling. 'Follow me if you want to see the Great Hall.'

There were shouts of assent all round, and everyone followed him round to the main door and into the enormous stone-walled, stone-floored Great Hall, watched only by the sightless eyes of the dozens of stags' heads mounted every few feet from each other in the upper walls. Phones and cameras buzzed and bleeped before Ross ushered them all out.

As they returned to the picnic site, Joyce said, 'We can't

possibly leave everything like this!' She was looking in dismay at the cluttered tables.

'Yes, you can,' Ally said. 'It won't be the earl or Magda who'll be washing these dishes.' At that moment Mrs Fraser, along with Mrs Jamieson, appeared to clear up. 'These two will have it tidy in no time.'

The two in question were already piling plates onto trays, Mrs Fraser saying, 'Ye'll only get in the way. Off with ye.'

As they wandered back down to the malthouse, Brigitte said, 'Well, it's for sure we aren't going to want any dinner tonight!'

'You're all very welcome to sit in the garden,' Ally said, 'although I must apologise that I haven't got round to doing much weeding lately.' It was half past six, but the sun was still warm.

As they entered through the gate, Joyce approached Ally. She looked around warily before she spoke. 'I've been wanting to have a quiet word with you all day but I haven't had the chance before. I think I know who killed Jodi Jones,' she said in little more than a whisper.

'Really? What makes you think that?' Ally asked.

'Something I found out this morning. I don't want it to be obvious that I'm talking to you now. I'll come down a bit earlier in the morning, after I've slept on it. But I'm pretty confident that I'm right.'

'Oh, Joyce!' Ally exclaimed. 'Can't you tell me *now*?'

Joyce shook her head and held a forefinger over her pursed lips. 'In the morning,' she repeated before rushing out to join the others in the garden.

Ally was deep in thought as she brought out cushions from the summerhouse and scattered them over the garden furniture. They'd had a long, winter hibernation, and she had to knock the cobwebs off first. She noticed that her guests had eagerly partaken of the earl's wine and were now looking decidedly sleepy.

As she returned to the house, Ally saw a woman walking up the drive and, as she neared, she recognised Laura.

'Oh, hello,' Ally greeted her. 'I'm afraid the picnic's over.' Ally knew now where Laura had most likely been but did not want to give her any indication of that.

Laura gave a brief smile. 'I just wondered where everyone was.'

'They're all stretched out in the garden, so why don't you join them? Have you had a nice afternoon?'

'Yes, thank you,' Laura replied politely before disappearing through the gate into the garden.

Ally shrugged as she re-entered the kitchen.

'Strange woman, that Laura,' she remarked later that evening to Ross. 'She doesn't say much, doesn't participate much, so it can only be Owen that's brought her up here. Wonder why she's suddenly shown up?'

'Come to kill again, I expect,' Ross said with a wicked grin.

'Be serious, Ross!' Ally thought for a moment. 'The earl is convinced it's Penelope and doesn't seem particularly horrified at the prospect. They greeted each other like old friends, which I suppose they are.'

'These aristos will always stick together,' Ross remarked. 'For my money, I thought that the Frenchwoman's husband was a little strange at times.'

'George?'

'Yes, George. What's he doing here anyway? I don't see any of the other husbands appearing.'

'I'm not altogether sure that the others *have* husbands,' Ally said thoughtfully. 'At least, not husbands that they're living with. So what was it about George that you thought to be strange?'

'He just looks a bit shifty sometimes, that's all. He was going on and on about how rubbishy Jodi Jones's books were, and how he could never bring himself to publish "that sort of thing".'

'But he hadn't arrived when Jodi was killed,' Ally pointed out.

'As far as you know,' said Ross, narrowing his eyes.

Ally giggled. 'Are you trying to tell me that he just walked into the Craigmonie, made his way to the ladies' cloakroom at the exact moment that Jodi was there, strangled her and walked out again, without ever bumping into any of the women who were having a pee or powdering their noses?'

'One of them was his wife, Brigitte,' Ross remarked. 'She could have been in on the act. In fact, she could be the killer.'

'I'll tell you something interesting,' Ally said. 'When we all got back from the castle, Joyce took me aside and told me she was pretty certain she knew who'd done it. She said she'd come down early in the morning to tell me, after she'd "slept on it", and she didn't want to be seen talking to me now.'

'Well, Ally, she could be trying to put you off the scent if it was herself. Who does she share a room with?' Ross asked.

'Millie, the little stocky one.'

'You've got to look out for little mousy ones! Appearances can be deceptive.'

'You're probably right,' Ally admitted. 'I saw her swimming in Loch Soular and had no idea she was such a powerful swimmer.'

'There you are then,' said Ross.

'Then, of course, there's Laura, my main suspect. The one who's having it off with Owen Jones and who suddenly appeared in the garden when everyone got back. What was that all about?'

Ross shook his head. 'Seems strange. What about Della?'

'She *was* the main suspect,' Ally reminded him.

'And then there's the Cornish one…'

'That's Morwenna, who's actually Welsh by birth. Her husband and Jodi had an affair years ago, but I think she was quite pleased to be rid of him.' Ally looked at her watch. 'It's nearly eight o'clock and I imagine they're all inside now, so I'll go and put the cushions away in case it rains overnight.'

Ross stood up. 'Let me help you.'

A couple of the roses, which had been in bud this morning, had now exploded out in all their beauty, one pink and one yellow, filling the air with their scent.

'Ooh, that perfume!' Ally said, sniffing the pink one. She looked around the garden and was about to pick up the first mattress when she was astonished to see Joyce fast asleep on one of the loungers underneath a rowan tree. 'Would you look at *her*!' she exclaimed.

'She looks very comfortable,' Ross agreed.

'She can't stay there all night,' Ally said, 'so I'm going to have to wake her up.'

She crossed the lawn to where Joyce was lying. 'Joyce?' she said quietly. Then, 'Hey, Joyce,' more loudly.

There was no response.

'A deep sleeper obviously,' Ross said, bending down and shouting, 'Wakey, wakey.'

There was still no response nor a glimmer of any reaction.

Ally was becoming concerned. 'Do you suppose she's all right?'

'Maybe her hearing's not good,' Ross said, looking a little worried too. 'Let's give her a shake.' He began to shake her gently, then more strongly.

They exchanged glances.

'I don't think this is normal,' Ally said. 'She should have woken up by now, for goodness' sake.'

Ross gently lifted one of her eyelids. 'Bloody hell,' he said, 'I think she's in a coma. We need an ambulance, Ally!'

THIRTEEN

The three Craigmonie residents had returned to their hotel, Brigitte and George had gone out somewhere or other, and the other two women had retired to their rooms to watch TV but now came rushing downstairs when they heard the ambulance arrive with sirens blaring.

'What do we know about this lady?' one of the paramedics asked as they lifted Joyce onto the stretcher.

'I can bring down her handbag, if that's any help?' Millie asked before rushing upstairs again.

'She was chatting away just a short time ago,' bawled an appalled Penelope. 'She seemed perfectly well, then.'

'I only know she's diabetic,' Ally said, 'and she doesn't drink alcohol.'

The paramedics exchanged glances. 'Could be an insulin overdose,' one of them said as they lifted the stretcher into the ambulance, having established her name, address and as many particulars as possible from her diary in her handbag.

'Better keep that safe upstairs, Millie,' Ross advised, indicating the handbag.

Ally was thankful he was there because he had taken

over, calmed the two women down and had phoned the Craigmonie to talk to Callum about the three women who were staying there. 'In case there's any suspicion of foul play, it's probably wise to make sure that none of them leave.' As he came off the phone, he said to Ally, 'This could be quite serious, bearing in mind what you said to me earlier.'

'I hope she's going to be all right,' Ally said as she watched the ambulance racing down the road, lights flashing, sirens blaring. 'Joyce was very careful about her diet so I can't believe she'd have got her insulin dose wrong.'

'Plainly she got it very wrong,' Ross remarked, then added, 'unless it was administered by someone else.'

'Oh God!' exclaimed Ally. 'I hadn't even thought of that!'

'Don't forget she was about to tell you who she thought the killer was,' Ross said.

'Do you think then that she, too, could be a victim of the killer if the killer suspected she was about to spill the beans?'

'Let's see what happens,' Ross said calmly. 'Hopefully she'll recover and be able to tell us what happened.'

Ally did not sleep well. She was feeling distracted, worrying so much that she could hardly set the breakfast table. Then, at the same time as her guests appeared for breakfast, so did Detective Inspector Amir Kandahar.

'Come into the kitchen, Amir,' Ally said, 'and I'll make you a tea. I'm just about to do breakfasts.'

The detective sat down at the far end of the kitchen table and removed a file from his briefcase. He cleared his throat and said, 'I'm really sorry to tell you this, but Joyce Williams died just after midnight from what appears to have been a massive overdose of insulin.'

'Oh, *no!*'

Ally began to cry, and Ross put his arm around her shoulders. 'How on earth could that happen?' he asked.

'She had to have been injected,' Amir said. 'Her body has been examined thoroughly, but it's difficult to diagnose because she obviously injects herself every day.'

'Yes, she kept her insulin in a box in my fridge,' Ally said, wiping her eyes.

'I'll need that box, please. And I need to know who might have had access to it.'

'Access!' Ally shook her head. 'Well, I suppose everyone had—'

'Everyone?' Amir frowned.

'Well, I don't lock the kitchen door, so anyone could have sneaked in there when I was out.'

'So anyone staying here could be a suspect?'

'Yes, of course. Are you saying that you think she's been murdered then?' Ally asked, thinking back in horror to her conversation of the previous evening. She accepted a handkerchief from Ross and gave her nose a blow. 'If that's true, then it must have been while she was lazing in the garden?' She handed Amir his tea distractedly.

Amir didn't reply for a moment. Then he said, 'I need to talk to you about that. I need to know who was with her yesterday evening and for how long. My officers are searching the garden and the surrounding area at this moment to see if they can find a syringe, just in case someone administered the drug in the garden and then threw away the syringe, so I apologise if we mess up some of your flower beds and pots.'

'I'll sort that out later,' Ross said to Ally, 'so don't you worry.'

'What about breakfasts?' Ally asked, looking towards the dining room.

No sooner had she spoken than Ross went straight in there

and emerged a minute later. 'All continental,' he said, 'because no one's feeling very hungry. I'll sort it.'

Ally wondered for the umpteenth time what on earth she'd do without Ross. She might consider herself to be a strong, independent woman, but on occasions like this, he was indispensable and endlessly supportive. As she placed some bread in the toaster for herself, she asked, 'What can we do now?'

Amir sipped his tea, phone at the ready. 'Just for a start we need a detailed account of everyone's movements yesterday evening. I hope you don't mind, but I've posted a policeman at your front door to prevent anyone from leaving, and likewise down at the hotel.'

Ally told him in as much detail as she could about the earl's picnic, and all the women sitting in the garden afterwards, including Laura, who had not actually gone to the picnic. What could have been Laura's reason for suddenly appearing out of the blue? Laura, who never normally joined in.

'There's something I haven't told you, Amir,' Ally said hesitantly. 'Laura Pike has been seen leaving Owen Jones's van in her underwear. She's almost certainly having an affair with Jodi's ex-husband.'

Amir pulled a face. 'That certainly could be a motive, and we really don't have much in the way of motives so far, do we? What about the Frenchwoman with the husband?' Amir asked. 'You said they went out yesterday evening?'

'Yes, but they only went out for a drink at the Craigmonie Bar, I believe,' Ally replied.

'And did they spend much time in your garden with the others before they went out?'

'Probably half an hour or so,' Ally said, racking her brain.

'Hmm,' said Amir. 'Do you have any idea how long they all remained in the garden together? Who left first? Who left last?'

Ally shook her head, looking at Ross, who'd rejoined them

now the breakfasts had been dealt with. 'We didn't go out to join them, did we? We left them to it until about eight o'clock when we went out to put away the cushions and found poor Joyce comatose.'

Amir nodded, and Ally noticed him looking questioningly at Ross.

'Sorry,' she added, 'I should have introduced you earlier. This is my friend, Ross Patterson, who was with me all day yesterday. And, Ross, as I'm sure you're aware by now, this is Detective Inspector Amir Kandahar.'

Both men smiled and nodded at each other.

'Are the remaining three women all in the dining room?' Amir asked.

Ally nodded, though she didn't much like the way he said 'remaining women' like they were being knocked off, one by one. *And then there were none!* 'I'll go and see them,' she added, standing up and making her way towards the door.

As she walked through the hall, she noticed a lone policeman standing guard outside the front door and wondered briefly if she should offer him a hot drink.

In the dining room, there was a buzz of conversation, everyone talking at once, then a lapse into silence when they saw Ally coming in.

'Can I get you anything else?' she asked, noticing that they seemed to be almost finished. 'More coffee? Tea?'

There was a general shaking of heads. 'What's going on out there?' asked George.

Ally realised that they hadn't yet heard the news. 'I'm really sorry to tell you that poor Joyce died in the hospital around midnight,' she said, feeling tears prickling her eyes again.

'*What?*'

'How?'

'Why?'

'So where do the police come into all this?' asked George.

'The inspector will tell you everything,' Ally said, aware that it wasn't her place to tell them anything.

'Well, plainly, the constabulary are not here for the good of their health,' boomed Penelope, wiping crumbs off her sweater. 'So who's going to be next, eh?' She looked round at the others. 'I'm not so sure now about staying on for another week.'

'We might not have the choice,' said Millie. 'Let's wait to see what the detective's going to say.'

'Thank God you are here, George,' murmured Brigitte, clasping his arm. 'I could not cope with this all on my own.' She bit into a croissant.

'We all left the garden about the same time last night,' Millie said, looking around, 'leaving Joyce asleep on the lounger because it seemed such a shame to wake her.'

At this point, Amir, armed with his phone and his briefcase, came through the door.

'Thanks, Ally,' he said, giving her a look which she took as a cue to leave.

The policeman at the door, when asked, said he could murder a cup of strong tea, then clapped his hand over his mouth and added, 'Perhaps that wasn't the most diplomatic way of asking?'

When Morag arrived to do the rooms she was bewildered to see police at the door and in the garden. 'What the hell's goin' on *now?*' she asked crossly.

Ally told her.

'Which woman was that? The diabetic one, or the wee one, or the loud one, or the madam with the husband?'

'The diabetic one. How did you know she was diabetic, Morag?'

'Because I saw her insulin in the fridge and the yellow sharps box in the bedroom where she puts her syringes after she'll have injected herself. I saw all that when I was cleaning. Murdo's brother's a diabetic, so I know the signs.'

'The police think she may have received an overdose of insulin,' Ally said, 'while she was asleep under the rowan tree.'

'Goodness me!' exclaimed Morag. 'At this rate, ye'll have naebody left!' She frowned. 'How am I supposed to do the rooms with them all hangin' about?'

'I don't know, Morag. Perhaps ask them – politely – if they'd be kind enough to wait in the sitting room while you do the cleaning?'

'What a bugger!' said Morag.

Her four remaining guests showed no inclination to go out. Ally had hoped they would as she fancied having a look in their bedrooms for any likely clues. Then she wondered if she was getting carried away with Rigby's praise for her detective abilities and she should leave it to the experts.

Ross and Ebony had gone home to welcome some guests who were due to arrive in his holiday cottages, Morag had done the bedrooms with a lot of muttering about guests being under her feet, and Ally had vacuumed downstairs and cleared the kitchen. She fancied calling in on her friend, Linda, to see how she was getting on with Callum and to pick up any news. She also needed some salt so decided to combine a visit to Linda with a visit to the village shop.

Ally had dreaded visiting the shop when she first arrived in Locharran, mainly due to Queenie's insatiable appetite for gossip, and Ally herself was at that time providing a fair bit of the gossip. Over the past year though, Queenie had almost begun to treat her as a local, which was praise indeed.

'Och!' said Queenie sadly. 'Ye're havin' a right old time of it up at the malthouse, Mrs McKinley.'

Ally nodded. 'I'm afraid you're right. Incidentally, why don't you call me Ally now that we know each other quite well?'

'That's an odd kinda name for a woman,' Queenie remarked, brushing some crumbs off the countertop.

'Well, it's short for Alison, but I've always been called Ally.'

Queenie nodded. 'What are ye wantin' then?'

'Just some salt, Queenie. Sea salt, please.'

'Over on the stand by the window,' said Queenie. She narrowed her eyes. 'So, who wiz murdered *this* time?'

Ally located the salt and placed it on the counter. 'The lady died of a diabetic coma, I believe, and we don't know anything more at this stage.'

'Our brother wiz diabetic,' Queenie said. Then she shouted, 'Our Charlie wiz diabetic, wizn't he, Bessie?'

There was no sign of Bessie and no reply. 'Well, he wiz. But he wiz fine until the bus hit him.'

'The *bus* hit him?' Ally repeated.

'Aye, the bus from Clachar. That wiz in the days when they ran a decent local bus service. That bus called at all the wee villages...'

'Your brother was hit by a *bus*?' Ally asked again.

'Ah *told* ye! The bus from Clachar! The driver, Ecky, wiz awful upset.'

'Well, he would be,' Ally said, 'but what about your brother?'

'Och, he was *flattened*. Flat as a flounder. Ye can see his grave if ye look in the churchyard, right near the gate.'

'So it killed him?' Ally asked, horrified.

'Of course it killed him – it wiz a big bus,' said Queenie, taking the money for the salt and depositing it in the till. 'But Charlie wid've been three sheets to the wind, so he probably widnae have felt much.' She sniffed. 'He liked a wee drink,' she added by way of explanation.

'How awful!' Ally said.

'Aye, but it wiz a *grand* funeral. Folks came from miles around. Now, would ye be needin' anythin' else, Mrs Mc— Ally?'

'Not just at the moment, thank you,' Ally replied, taking her leave.

'You must have a slice of my rum, coconut and pineapple cake,' Linda said as she placed a cup of tea in front of Ally.

'Rum, coconut and pineapple?'

'It's a kind of a pina colada cake, you see. I'm trying to bring a touch of the exotic into the lives of Locharran residents!' Linda grinned.

'Well, you've certainly succeeded,' Ally replied as she took an experimental bite. 'This is something else – wow!'

'Oh good,' said Linda. 'I'm glad you like it. It's going down a storm at the Craigmonie.'

'I'm not at all surprised!' Ally said, taking a larger bite.

'Never mind the cake,' said Linda. 'What's all this about someone being taken away from the malthouse in an ambulance last night?'

Ally sighed. 'I'm afraid it's true. She was a nice lady called Joyce – Joyce Williams. But she was diabetic and fell into a coma.' She hesitated, then decided to tell Linda just what had happened. 'She died in hospital later.'

'Oh no!' Linda looked horrified.

'They suspect foul play because it was due to an overdose of insulin,' Ally explained. 'But what really worries me is that Joyce was about to tell me something. I think she was convinced she knew who the killer was.'

'So you're suggesting that she may have been silenced by someone?'

'I rather fear she may have been.' Ally sighed, then ate some more cake. 'God, Linda, this thing is delicious!'

'So where did this happen? In her bedroom?'

Ally explained about the picnic and them all lazing in the garden afterwards. 'It's the same old story – it could have been any one of them. Apparently, Joyce fell asleep.'

'But surely someone would be seen if they injected her or something?'

'Joyce kept her insulin in my fridge in the kitchen, so any one of them could have sneaked in there at some time, I suppose. It's all very scary. How's Callum coping with the three women staying there?'

Linda shook her head. 'He's going nuts. The police keep appearing, much to the consternation of the other guests. And he keeps wittering on about the hotel's wonderful reputation, and how there's never been any scandal until now.' She refilled the teacups. 'But at least one of the women looks like being cleared and allowed to go home.'

'*What?*' Ally nearly dropped her cup. 'Which one?'

Linda shrugged. 'Can't honestly remember what he said.'

'I must go in to see him straight away,' Ally said, draining her cup.

'I wouldn't bother if I were you because he's had to go to Inverness today. But, listen, why don't we all go out somewhere as a foursome and you can ask him then?'

'Dinner at Seascape perhaps?' Ally suggested.

'Brilliant idea!' exclaimed Linda. 'What are you doing tonight?'

'Nothing that I know of,' Ally admitted. 'I'm sure Ross would be more than happy to go there.'

'OK, I'll call them now and book a table for four,' Linda said. 'Shouldn't be a problem on a Monday evening.'

As she made her way home, Ally tried to work out which of the Craigmonie suspects could possibly have been cleared. Della – unlikely, as she was the most likely suspect surely. Laura – who could tell with Laura? Strange lady. That left Morwenna, of course. She had seemed the least likely to Ally, but she had to admit that she really hadn't a clue. What sort of sleuth was *she*, who couldn't even choose between three women, never mind six?

FOURTEEN

The evenings were light now, and the view from Seascape was spectacular. As the name implied, the seafood restaurant was situated on a clifftop overlooking the sea and the craggy coastline, with stunning views out towards the islands. The tourists hadn't arrived in force yet, but the restaurant was still two-thirds full, even on a Monday evening.

'I expected it to be empty,' Ross said as the waiter apologised for not having a table vacant at the window.

'Just shows how popular this place is,' Ally agreed.

'It's so good to get right away from Locharran for a few hours,' Callum said with a sigh. 'I've left Ivan in charge, so hopefully I won't be missed.'

Ivan was the Craigmonie's Lithuanian barman who, ten years previously, had come to Locharran as a backpacking student and decided to stay, partly because of his love for the area but more accurately for his love of Locharran whisky, which he imbibed daily and frequently.

After they'd ordered their food and poured out some wine, Ally said casually, 'I hear that one of your women suspects has been cleared to go home, Callum?'

Callum nodded. 'Still two to go,' he said cheerfully.

'But *who*?' Ally asked. 'Who was cleared to go?'

'The red-haired Irish one – Delia, Della, whatever her name was,' Callum replied.

'Della Moran? But she was the *chief* suspect!' Ally exclaimed, astonished. 'How come?'

'Well,' said Callum, 'while Jodi Jones was in the bar knocking back a double Scotch immediately after the disruption in the Garden Room, this bloke started chatting her up. Ivan witnessed this, and we've been looking for the man ever since. Luckily, he came back into the bar last night and told us what had happened. Apparently, he was suddenly riveted by the sight of this "red-haired beauty" – *his* words, not mine – going into the ladies' room, which you can see quite clearly along the corridor from the bar. Ivan was listening in, and the bloke said something like, "Wow! Where did *she* come from?" Jodi then snapped that she was the woman who'd caused the disruption, and that she was a nasty liar. Nevertheless, the bloke kept watching until he saw Della coming out again and re-enter the Garden Room, although he'd continued chatting to Jodi.'

'He sounds a delightful type,' Linda said acidly.

'Doesn't he just!' agreed Ally.

'Well, whatever you think of him, he did have the decency to contact the police after he heard about Jodi's murder,' Callum said.

'And?' Ally asked as the waiter approached with their starters.

'When he got out to the car park, he could see Della through the French windows, in the middle of a group of women,' Callum continued.

Ally was still confused as she tackled her lobster bisque. 'So what exactly are you saying?'

'It was confirmed that Della was the first to visit the cloakroom – the *only* time she visited the cloakroom, which was verified by the others – and while Jodi was in the bar. Confirmed by Ivan, who took a keen interest in the whole thing. So, much as she may have wanted to, Della Moran did not kill Jodi Jones.'

'And now she's been allowed to go home?' Ally asked.

'Yes, she's gone,' Callum confirmed.

Linda was also looking confused. 'So who's still staying at the hotel?' she asked Callum.

'A woman from Bristol and a woman from Cornwall,' Callum replied, 'neither of whom are particularly interesting.'

'It's the dull ones you have to watch out for!' Ross said cheerfully.

'That's Laura and Morwenna,' Ally said. Then to herself she added, 'Plus Millie, Penelope and Brigitte.' Five women! She knew that she needed, somehow or other, to get chatting to them individually because there just had to be a clue there somewhere.

'You're really keen to solve this, aren't you, Ally?' Linda asked, studying her.

'Yes, I am,' Ally replied firmly. 'Apart from anything else I need to know if I'm harbouring a murderer under my roof, and I'd like to know when I can take bookings for guests again.'

But the main reason, Ally thought, was to find out, for Rigby's sake, who had killed his sister and why? Jodi Jones certainly did appear to be his long-lost sister, right down to the birthmark, but this information could not be made public. Apart from telling Ross, of course. Ally couldn't risk anyone, accidentally or otherwise, passing on the information and so blighting Rigby's chances of eventually solving the case himself.

The conversation then turned to other things, and Ally was glad of the distraction. Not least because she was thrilled to see the bond that had developed between Linda and Callum.

Could there be another wedding on the horizon? she wondered.

. . .

Ally and Ross got back to the malthouse at precisely the same time as Brigitte and George.

'We were at the Craigmonie for a meal,' Brigitte said, 'but have you heard the *latest*?' She licked her lips. 'Della Moran has been cleared and is probably swanning around Derry as we speak!'

'Yes, we had heard,' Ally said, glancing at Ross, who was looking exhausted and ready for bed.

'So this narrows it down to just five of us,' Brigitte added, 'and I can tell you, right now, that it was not me!'

'It wasn't Brigitte,' George confirmed fondly, looking towards the stairs.

'I've no doubt the inspector will be questioning everyone again, *tomorrow*,' Ross said.

Brigitte stayed put. 'Well, I don't think it's fair,' she said with a pout. 'I'm sure Della must have gone to the loo again later.'

'Apparently she didn't,' Ally said, 'and that's been proved, otherwise the inspector would not have permitted her to leave.'

'She *hated* Jodi,' Brigitte went on, 'and she told me so.'

'That doesn't make her the killer,' Ross said, yawning. 'If you don't mind, I'm knackered and I'm off to bed.' He looked hopefully at Ally.

'You and me both,' agreed George, heading towards the main staircase.

'I want a little word with Ally,' said Brigitte. 'Just for a moment.'

Ally shepherded her into the sitting room, wondering what was coming.

'I know that you're *friendly* with the inspector,' Brigitte said as she plonked herself in the middle of the sofa, 'so I think you should tell him that Penelope is very strange.'

'She *is*?' Ally asked, amazed.

Brigitte nodded. 'Did you know she'd once been suspected of murder? And she was in prison for another crime?'

'Really?' In spite of being tired and ready for bed, Ally was suddenly awake and curious.

'More than once!' Brigitte said triumphantly.

'When?' Ally asked.

'Many years ago. When she was young.'

'So what did she do?'

'She tried to stab a man who was pressing himself upon her,' Brigitte replied.

'How do you know this?' Ally asked.

'Because I googled her and then found out her name before she was married, and then I googled *that* name.'

Ally cursed herself for not having done precisely that and wondered if Amir had.

'And then this Penelope, some years ago, was accused of killing her husband! *Her husband!*' Brigitte repeated triumphantly.

'I think the police are aware of that,' Ally said, 'but she was freed due to lack of evidence.'

'Once a killer, always a killer!' said Brigitte sanctimoniously.

'*If* she was a killer,' said Ally.

But Brigitte wasn't finished yet. 'And then there is Millie,' she said.

'What about Millie?' Ally asked.

'Millie shared a bedroom with Joyce and so she must have had access to the insulin, yes? So, she must be the most likely person to kill Joyce!'

'But she and Joyce got on well,' Ally said. 'Anyone could have got the insulin because it was in my fridge in the kitchen.'

Brigitte shrugged. 'There is some connection there. There must be! It must have been one of them.'

'That doesn't seem to be much of a reason, Brigitte, as far as

Millie's concerned. And you've just said that you think Penelope was the killer.'

Brigitte was nowhere near finished yet. 'What I mean is that anyone could have done it. That Laura! Tell me, where does she go when we socialise? Why is she here? She must go somewhere, no?'

'Perhaps she's just a loner?' Ally suggested, stifling a yawn, determined not to mention what she knew.

'Why then does she come up here to Scotland with a group of women?'

'To improve her writing ability?' Ally suggested. 'Isn't that why you're all here?'

Brigitte shook her head. 'No, I think one of us came here to kill.' She paused. 'Why did she appear here after we all got back from the picnic – eh? And I wonder about this Morwenna too! She tells me that Jodi once stole her husband. Her *husband!* Would you not be angry?'

'I wouldn't be pleased exactly,' admitted Ally with a smile, thinking of anyone trying to steal poor old Ken! Years ago, though, maybe... 'That was a long time ago, and surely if she wanted to kill Jodi, she'd have done it then? Brigitte, you're not really telling me much that I don't know already.'

'Well,' said Brigitte, standing up, 'I hope most sincerely that you do not suspect *me!*'

'It's not my business to suspect anyone. That's the job of the police.' Ally hesitated for a moment. 'I am a little curious though why you were looking through Jodi's diary, particularly at the page on which she'd written something about having a chat with you?'

Brigitte froze, her eyes wide. 'How could you possibly know that? I tore out the page.'

'I know you did, but I saw the imprint of her writing on the page beneath.'

Brigitte appeared suddenly uncertain. 'I'd written to Jodi

two weeks ago and she'd promised we'd have a chat.' Brigitte added, 'My husband is a publisher. We publish wonderful books. Reference books, language books, dictionaries, thesauruses, instruction books, religious books, and there was something I wanted to ask her – purely on a literary note.' She pulled a face. 'We do not, of course, publish the kind of books that she wrote.'

'So why then are you here, Brigitte?'

'Because she is *published!* And I want to be published too, Ally! I wanted to know her secrets, her tips, her ideas! But one of these other women is not here for that reason.'

Ally stifled a yawn. 'You may be right, but I hope you don't mind if I go to bed now?'

Brigitte nodded. 'It has been good to talk to you,' she said as she made her way towards the main staircase.

Ally switched off the lights and headed towards her own staircase behind the kitchen. She knew that Ross would probably be asleep, and he was.

As she lay in bed, she thought that Brigitte had a reason for everyone to kill Jodi, except herself. Was she hiding something? What had she really been looking for in Room 1? Did this woman protest too much?

FIFTEEN

Shortly after the women had finished breakfast the next morning, Ally went to clear away the breakfast dishes and found Millie still in the dining room.

'Oh, sorry, Millie. I thought everyone had gone upstairs.'

'No, no, I've finished breakfast, but I wanted to ask you about buses. I'm having a day off from writing and thought I'd make a trip to Inverness. To buy a hat.'

'A *hat*?'

Millie looked a little embarrassed. 'Yes, I'd like to wear a hat to Jodi Jones's funeral, out of respect, you know. I really did admire her such a lot.'

'Well, that's certainly very respectful, Millie, but I'm not sure that people wear hats so much to funerals these days.' Ally paused, then added, 'I don't think that Jodi's funeral is going to be exactly *formal*.'

'I'm not bothered what people do or don't do,' Millie said firmly. 'I am going to wear a hat.'

Feeling somewhat chastened, Ally said, 'Yes, yes, of course. Let's see if there are any bus timetables left in the hall, but I do know there's one which stops outside the Craigmonie every morning at around half past nine, which would get you into town around eleven thirty. How does that sound?'

'That sounds perfect,' Millie replied as she headed towards the stairs. 'Thanks so much.'

As she carried a tray of dishes into the kitchen, Ally wondered about the hat. She herself had no intention of wearing a hat. Knowing what the westerly winds were like in this part of the world, any hat would need to be well anchored into position or it would be back in Inverness faster than the bus. She hoped Millie would think to buy some hatpins.

She'd barely had time to load the dishwasher when Amir Kandahar appeared again.

For the umpteenth time, Ally wondered if she should tell him about Jodi Jones being Rigby's missing sister. She'd promised Rigby she wouldn't, but what if that information proved to be vital to the case?

Amir sat down, the file on his knee and said that, yes, he'd love a mug of tea. 'Perhaps it'll help me to focus more clearly on this case.'

'What's almost certain,' Ally said, 'is that whoever killed Joyce did so to stop her telling me about some proof she had regarding who killed Jodi.'

Amir stared at her in amazement. 'She *knew* something?'

'Yes, I should have mentioned it yesterday, but I was so upset I forgot. Joyce thought she did,' Ally replied, handing him his mug of tea. 'She intended to tell me yesterday morning and planned to come down early to avoid being overheard.'

'And you have no idea what it might have been that she wanted to tell you?'

Ally shook her head. 'None at all.'

'If she was correct in her assumption, then we have a motive for her death,' said Amir, then added, '*If.*'

'Do you know if Jodi had any children?' Ally asked, half

hoping he did so that she didn't need to keep feeling so guilty about the information she was keeping from him.

'None that we know of yet,' Amir replied. 'There's been plenty of press coverage of Jodi Jones's death, so, if there's any around, they're bound to know. The husband's arranged all the burial details, according to her express wishes. She'd told him she wanted to be buried close to where she died, to spare the environment as much as possible and have a humanist send-off.' Amir rolled his eyes. 'And in accordance with Jodi's wishes, Owen Jones has purchased a burial plot at a natural burial site in the middle of nowhere, near Brodale.'

Ally nodded, though she'd heard this already from Ross.

'So the police are releasing her body?' Ally asked.

'Yes, on Thursday, in a wicker coffin.'

'That seems quite speedy,' she said.

'Yes. Cause of death is strangulation, and there are no fingerprints or DNA whatsoever, although we are keeping the scarf. She was killed at the washbasins and then dragged across the floor and dumped in the out-of-order toilet cubicle. It was genuinely out of order because the flush didn't work.' Amir drank some tea. 'I'd really like this all sorted out before the funeral,' he added.

'What? Before *Sunday*?'

He nodded. 'Have you had a chance to speak to any of the women individually?'

'Only Brigitte last night,' Ally replied. 'She was giving me reasons why everyone could be guilty – apart from herself, of course. And she wasn't much impressed with Jodi's novels.'

'So why is she here?' Amir asked. 'She's told me she's writing women's fiction too, so why does she consider herself to be so superior?'

'Well, as I told you before, she did have a meeting arranged with Jodi. Brigitte explained that it was about something that she'd written to Jodi about beforehand – she wanted to know how to get published.' Then she added, 'I also had a chance to have a quick chat with Millie the other evening, when I took my dog for a walk up to Loch Soular and found her swimming – Olympic standard! – up and down the loch, which is quite a distance.'

'Did she appear to have any connection with Jodi Jones?' Amir asked.

'No, but she wasn't at all forthcoming about her private life, other than that she loves swimming.' Ally thought for a moment. 'She's not very tall, but she's got strong shoulders.'

'So has Mrs Fortescue-Rawlins,' said Amir. 'I don't think that necessarily makes them stranglers. Thanks for your help, Ally, but I must be off.'

After Amir had gone, Ally went over things in her mind and kept recalling her conversation with Desdemona when she'd initially made the booking and mentioned that she and Jodi had been at university together. How could that have been possible if Jodi was Joanne Rigby? She realised she must talk to Desdemona again before she said anything to Rigby himself, but she baulked at the thought of driving all the way up to Desdemona's place at Loch Trioch, along that treacherous road, and the possible damage that the rough track could make to the underside of her car. She decided to try phoning.

'Yes?' Desdemona barked in her usual terse manner.

'Hi, it's Ally. I just wanted to ask you some more about Jodi Jones and your time at university together, and wondered if you might be coming down to Locharran in the next day or two?'

'Not if I can help it,' Desdemona replied. 'I'm very busy in my garden at the moment. What did you want to know?'

'I'm just trying to piece together some information about Jodi,' Ally said, 'because she fascinates me.' Ally realised that sounded a bit lame and wondered if Desdemona would believe her excuse.

'I can't think why,' Desdemona replied sharply, 'since she's no longer with us. I've told you already that we were quite friendly at university.'

'I just wondered if you knew anything about her background?' Ally asked, feeling she might as well get straight to the point.

'Can't remember,' Desdemona said. 'Don't think she spoke about it much. I only saw her at classes, never in the holidays. She was called Jo in those days, but I don't remember what her surname was then.'

'Did she seem to struggle moneywise?' Ally asked.

'We were *all* struggling moneywise!' said Desdemona. 'Even though university was free back then and we got grants to live on if we needed them. Still, we had to eat and drink, and she certainly liked a drink!'

'But can you remember where she lived or anything?' Ally persisted.

'Can't think why you're so interested.' There was a pause. 'I think she lived in Somerset or Dorset or somewhere like that, not in London. Hang on, I can remember something now. She told me she'd once been homeless for some reason but had been living with some older man, supposedly "doing his housekeeping" so that she could sit her A levels and get to university. She was desperate to be a writer.'

'Did you ever see the man?' Ally asked.

'Don't know if it was him but some guy with a big car used to pick her up at the end of term.'

'What did he look like?'

'I was never introduced to him, and I assumed he was the guy she lived with. Or whatever.'

Ally was becoming increasingly interested. 'But she

couldn't still be working for him if she was at university, could she?'

'No idea. But they always embraced,' Desdemona said.

'A lover's embrace? A fatherly embrace?'

'Ally, I've no bloody idea! I was never that close to them. Now I've got to go because I'm in the middle of planting my beans. Got to get going while the weather's so good.'

'Oh, sorry if I've—' Ally realised that she'd hung up.

She pondered over what little Desdemona had told her. Jodi had gone to 'keep house' for some man so that she could study and go to university. Hmm, Ally doubted the 'housekeeping' bit. Had that man, whoever he was, become a lover perhaps? In which case did he sponsor her education? Was it the same man who picked her up in his big car and embraced her? He certainly didn't sound like Owen Jones, whoever he was. And if she'd been pregnant, was he the father, and where was the baby?

Jodi had plainly been a survivor, whatever else she was. Until she came to Locharran...

Later, before the women, including Millie, now back from Inverness, set off for their dinner at the Craigmonie, Ally asked her, 'Did you have a good day's shopping?'

'Yes, I got exactly what I wanted,' said Millie. 'Very scenic journey.'

The others all looked at her with interest, but Millie was saying no more.

SIXTEEN

Ally hadn't had much time to herself over the past couple of days, and she'd become aware of the fact that she should really have been doing some research into Jodi Jones. There just might be some clue in there, somewhere, regarding her past life. Something that she could relay to Rigby at the very least.

She googled 'Jodi Jones' and then clicked meticulously on each website listed under her name. She was English; she wrote bestselling novels; she'd always wanted to write. She was a university graduate, specialising in Creative Writing, and she edited people's manuscripts. She had been married once, had lived in a commune in Wales for a few years, but was now single again, although rumour had it that there had never been a divorce and she was still in a relationship with her agent, Harry Harper, who, years ago, had left his wife and baby for her, creating much negative publicity.

But at the very foot of the page of search results was an online magazine called *Celebrity Confessions*. The very title indicated that it was bound to be full of lightweight rubbish, but why then, Ally wondered, was it listed under Jodi Jones? Worth a look, she thought.

After some clicking and re-clicking, Ally was finally able to bring the magazine up on the screen. Predictably, there were pages devoted to media personalities who'd had their love lives blighted one way or the other, their busts enlarged/reduced, and their Botox wonderful/gone wrong. Ally waded through the pages and then, there in the very centre was *AN INTERVIEW WITH THE FAMOUS WRITER OF WOMEN'S FICTION – JODI JONES. HER HEARTBREAKING STORY! EXCLUSIVE!*

Agog, Ally continued to read:

Jodi Jones confided to us that, back in August 1975 she gave birth to a baby. 'I wasn't yet seventeen,' she told us, 'and I've never told anyone this before.' At this point, Jodi had to dry her eyes. 'My family were somewhat strait-laced, right was right, wrong was wrong, and I most definitely was wrong. Abandoned by my family, I found a hostel for unmarried mothers and, immediately after the birth, they arranged adoption. So, that's what I did.' Jodi wiped her tears away again. 'I had my beautiful baby adopted.' She then described the heartbreak, and at a time when she was barely more than a child herself. 'It was a disgrace back then, but since then I've got married, lived in a commune and now I'm independent again. I admit that I've used men to get where I am today, top of the bestsellers' list. But do you know what? There was not a single day when I didn't think about my child. And then, one day, my child got in touch! Can you imagine? I got my motherhood back! And I don't intend to ever lose it again!

The reporter had added a further paragraph.

Jodi, has, for many years now, been in a well-publicised relationship with Harry Harper, her agent, the man who sent her on her way. He is known for having furthered the careers of several prominent female writers but had never become roman-tically involved with one before. What was particularly tragic was the fact that Harry Harper had left his wife heartbroken, and with a three-month-old baby, to move in with Jodi.

'What do you think, Ross?' Ally asked later as she showed him her findings on the laptop. 'It was a disgrace back then to become pregnant if you weren't married, and she seems to have spent her life being obsessed with having to give her baby away. What strikes me as being particularly sad is that she's admitted to "using" men after that, like she blamed *all* men for her own downfall, which it was then, of course, and her struggle for survival. But survive she did! She was completely unmoved by her lover leaving his wife and baby behind, which seems incredible. She may not have been a particularly nice woman, but she'd obviously become hardened by her experiences.'

'What I don't understand is why this child, if they exist, hasn't got in touch?' Ross said. 'I mean, Jodi's murder has been well reported by the media, and since there doesn't appear to have been any further offspring, then surely they'd be the heir to her considerable bank balance?'

'I think I should tell Amir, and Rigby, what I've found,' Ally said.

'I'm amazed they haven't discovered this for themselves,' Ross commented with a frown.

'Ah, but very few men would be likely to read the rubbish magazine that I waded through,' Ally said with a grin.

'Obviously we're not persistent enough,' Ross agreed.

On Wednesday morning, shortly after the women had gone out and Ross had gone home, Amir Kandahar put in an appearance again.

'It has been officially confirmed,' he said, 'that Joyce

Williams died of a massive overdose of insulin, as I suspected. We've checked the syringes you had stored in the box in your fridge and it appeared – assuming she brought sufficient for a week or two – that a quantity was missing.'

'Well, as I told you, almost anyone could have gone into the kitchen,' Ally admitted. 'I lock the outside doors if I'm going anywhere, but there's no lock on the kitchen door and all the women have keys so they can come and go as they wish.' She sighed. 'I think you're going to need a cup of tea.'

'I certainly do!' Amir frowned. 'So any one of them could have gone in there and helped themselves if you weren't around?'

'Yes, I guess so. But, Amir, I have something important to tell you. Jodi Jones had a child.'

'How come I have no record of this?' Amir asked, looking perplexed.

'Apparently it was adopted as a baby and didn't contact her until they were an adult.' Ally fired up her laptop and, after a few minutes, produced the magazine and the centre pages for his perusal.

Amir read it carefully as Ally made the tea, and then appeared to reread it, his eyes widening. 'I'm going to look into this,' he said, clicking several times on the article and noting down the website address. He looked up. 'Well, if she and her offspring are now as close as she's making out here, then where is he or she? Why haven't they appeared?'

'Good question,' Ally agreed.

'Is this a reputable magazine?' Amir asked.

'Not very. But don't you think she'd have sued if they printed something that was wrong? I mean, this was published a year ago.'

Ally handed him a mug and reached for the biscuit tin. 'Some shortbread?'

Amir nodded distractedly and helped himself to a generous

piece. 'You'd have to be on a bloody desert island or somewhere not to be aware of Jodi Jones's murder! So why has this child not appeared?' he asked again.

Ally shook her head.

'This thing is beginning to keep me awake at night,' Amir added with a sigh.

'You and me both,' said Ally. She longed to tell him about Rigby's long-lost sister, but a promise was a promise. Perhaps, though, she might now be able to persuade Rigby to tell Amir. Surely they were working towards the same goal? And it certainly didn't look like Rigby was likely to be back on the case any time soon.

Amir munched his shortbread for a moment, took a swig of tea and then asked out of the blue, 'Have you got a daughter?'

Taken aback for a moment, Ally replied, 'Yes, I have.'

'I have two,' said Amir, gazing out of the window. 'Their mother died two years ago.'

Ally had heard something similar from Rigby. 'I'm so sorry,' she said sincerely.

'She was a good mother,' Amir said, still gazing out of the window. 'But my girls are now teenagers. They're fifteen and seventeen, and it's not easy being the father of teenagers these days, Ally.'

'I know that,' Ally said, recalling countless arguments with both Jamie and Carol about what was allowed and what was not. 'Who looks after them when you're working?'

'My mother and my sister.' He sighed. 'My mother's nearly eighty and she's had ten children, but she doesn't understand this modern world. Do you know what I mean?'

Ally nodded.

'She doesn't understand technology, or the temptations and pitfalls of social media. Then there's my sister, who has a family of her own and can only give them limited time. They need their mother.'

Ally touched his arm. 'Oh, Amir, I'm sorry. It must be very difficult. But do you know what? My daughter, Carol, was an absolute nightmare! Boys, alcohol, drugs, you name it. My late husband was convinced she'd end up in prison, but I never lost hope. I had a feeling she'd come through it and come good, and do you know what? She did! Even after she and a friend once spent a night in a police cell for causing a disturbance of the peace. We were absolutely humiliated! Then off she went to London, got a job designing fabrics. She was always very arty-crafty. She married an airline pilot, has three kids and now lives a very conventional life in a leafy English village. So there you are! Never give up hope. I'm sure your two will come through this teenage bit, and I'm sure they've inherited your genes and will be decent, caring adults.'

'You're a very kind lady, Ally,' Amir said as he drained his tea. 'Thank you for listening to me because this has nothing whatsoever to do with the Jodi Jones case.'

After Amir had left, Ally removed the board from the wall and stared at it for a moment or two. How long was it since she'd studied it last? And how things had changed!

First of all, she must remove Della and poor Joyce. The main suspect still appeared to be Laura, at twelve o'clock, the chief suspect. Brigitte needed to be brought up to one o'clock, and Penelope should be lowered to six. She could find no reason for Penelope to be involved at all, other than her one-time unproven criminal record. Likewise Millie. Millie the Mouse! Ally seemed to recall, from years back, a film called *The Mouse That Roared*, so Millie might just roar yet. You could never tell. Just in case she did unexpectedly bellow, Ally placed her at seven o'clock, next to Penelope at six. Morwenna, she decided, could remain at five o'clock.

'You're absolutely sure that it was Laura you saw coming

out of Owen's van?' Ally asked Ross for the umpteenth time. And also for the umpteenth time, Ross replied, 'I've told you – I only saw Laura at a distance a couple of times, but there's no one in the village that matches that description or is likely to have any connection with Jodi's husband. I mean, they were both having affairs left, right and centre, weren't they? And as you keep telling me, Laura doesn't socialise with the others.' He squeezed Ally's arm. 'If you want to be certain, then you'll have to hide in the shrubs, and watch for her coming and going.'

'Do you think I should?' Ally asked doubtfully.

Ross sighed. 'No, I don't. But I know you well enough by now that you won't be happy until you do.'

Ally looked at her watch. 'I mean *everything* points to Laura. But I suppose it could be some other woman who's come to join him. What do you think?'

'I'll tell you what,' Ross continued, 'we'll go down to my place and, while I'm looking after the dogs and slaving away in my kitchen preparing a cordon bleu dinner for us, you can be peeking out of the bushes with your phone at the ready.' He laughed, plainly convinced that this was something of a joke.

'OK,' said Ally. 'I'll do that.'

Ally had been crouching in the bushes for almost an hour and had cramp in the muscles of the calf of her left leg. She clenched and unclenched her toes in the hope of alleviating the pain, trying not to scream, and was just about to limp her way back to Ross's barn when she heard footsteps.

And there was Laura, and it was *definitely* Laura, approaching Owen's scruffy abode. Then Owen appeared, with a smile on his face – that in itself was a sight that Ally had never yet witnessed – and he was embracing her. No. Not embracing, more like *devouring* her! There was little doubt that they were pleased to see each other.

Ally waited until they'd collapsed happily into the van before making her way back through the shrubbery to Ross's barn.

'Are you happy now?' he asked as he chopped up some garlic.

Ally nodded. 'Yes, yes I am.' At least she now had some news to pass on to Rigby, even if it was only the fact that his sister's husband was having an affair with a woman booked on the course which, in itself, was very suspicious. Or should she tell him this?

Ally could only hope that Rigby was still in the hospital because she had no idea where to find him otherwise.

'You've got me just in time,' he said when she finally managed to reach him on the phone in Ward 8. 'I'm being released today.' He paused for a moment. 'Have you been able to find out anything?'

'I've unearthed a few very interesting bits and pieces,' Ally replied. 'Although I'm not sure if they're particularly relevant or not. Still, I want to tell you. Shall I do so on the phone?'

'I'd prefer it if you told me in person,' he said after a moment. 'I'm going home just as soon as my medication arrives, and my wife is on her way to pick me up. Can I give you my address? Is there any chance you could visit me? Am I asking too much of you?'

'No, Bob, I'd be happy to visit you. Would it be OK if I came with Ross?'

'Of course it would be OK!' Rigby exclaimed. 'I'd be honoured, and so would Cathy, my wife. Have you got a pen? Good. Here's the address...'

. . .

'We'll go tomorrow and make a day of it,' Ross said later. 'We'll lunch at Drumnadrochit or somewhere and then continue on to Inverness and Rigby.'

Ally was pleased. Ross had a big, comfortable car, and he drove considerably faster than she did. Not only that, she was beginning to feel really tired, due not only to her advanced years but also to the stress of everything that was taking place around her.

Morag, fortunately, adored dogs, so Ally knew she'd be likely to agree to staying on for an extra hour or two. She knew exactly what Morag would do: leave the back door open for the dogs to romp around the garden, drink endless mugs of tea and sit spellbound in front of the television to catch up on all her favourite soaps.

'Oh aye,' Morag said with much sighing, to indicate that this was quite a chore. 'I might be able to manage that.'

They had lunch in Drumnadrochit, as planned, and Ally was able to have a large glass of wine which would doubtless facilitate the conversation she was about to have with Rigby.

Number 15, The Drive, was a white L-shaped bungalow with a newly painted, very glossy green front door. The front garden was neat and well weeded and boasted a collection of gnomes in one corner.

The door was opened by Cathy, who was a tiny, curvy lady with immaculate blonde hair and wearing a rather tight floral-print dress.

'Well,' she said, after studying them for a moment, 'you must be Ally and...'

'Ross,' he supplied, shaking her hand.

'Aye, Ross, that's it. Come on in.' She beamed as she stood aside to let them enter a tiny hall, which had a picture rail near the top of the walls, on which were displayed innumerable china plates. 'Come on into the lounge,' she said, 'and see himself.' She opened the door into a sea of floral chintz.

Rigby was sitting by the fireside in a bluebell-patterned armchair, wearing a snazzy red pullover, cord trousers and tartan slippers. Ally had only ever seen him formally dressed before so she took a moment to digest that this really *was* Rigby.

'You are *not* to stand up!' Cathy instructed him. 'Ally and Ross will understand.'

Ally and Ross nodded obediently as they settled themselves in the sea of pink roses and blue hydrangeas which covered the sofa opposite.

'It was good of you to come,' Rigby said. 'I know you're both busy.'

'It's good to see you looking so much better,' Ally said truthfully. 'How are you feeling?'

'Oh, much better, thanks. It's so good to get out of hospital and away from hospital food.' He looked fondly at his wife. 'Cathy's a great cook you know.'

'I'll just go and make some tea,' said Cathy, turning a little pink with the compliment.

As she left the room, Rigby asked, 'How are you getting on with Amir Kandahar?'

'Very well,' Ally replied. Then she added, 'I would like to be able to tell him about your sister, Bob.'

He pulled a face. 'Hmm, maybe. Have you managed to find out anything of interest?'

At this point, Cathy bustled in with a tray of tea, along with a large Victoria sponge, and set about pouring the tea into dainty china cups, having asked everyone how they liked it. She then insisted they all had a slice of the cake. 'I only baked it this morning,' she said.

Ally cleared her throat. 'Is it OK to tell you what I found?' She glanced in Cathy's direction.

'Oh, Cathy's well aware of everything,' Rigby said as Cathy nodded.

'Well,' Ally said, 'it appears that Jodi Jones gave birth to a baby in 1975 but had it adopted.' She removed her laptop from her bag, opened up the relevant page and passed the machine across to Rigby. 'You need to read this, Bob.'

'This sister business has taken over his life,' Cathy said, 'and the sooner it's all sorted out the better.' She sniffed loudly. 'There are times when I wish we'd never left Birmingham. You expect some crime in a big city, but you don't expect it up here, do you? And you certainly don't expect to find the body of your sister, *if* it is his sister.'

'The only way you're going to know for sure,' Ross said, 'is to request a DNA test.'

Rigby handed Ally back her laptop. 'I was in such a state of shock when I found her body that I didn't think to...' His voice drained away for a moment. 'If this stuff is true, then I must have a niece or nephew somewhere.'

'Surely it must be true,' Ally said, 'because this was printed over a year ago and so Jodi would have had plenty time to sue them for writing lies. But why hasn't the child, now an adult of course, appeared yet? Or the father of that child, if he's still alive? It seems that she was very much involved with her agent, Harry Harper.'

'Did you speak to Desdemona Morton again?' Rigby asked.

'Yes, on the phone. She only knew Jodi at university and had no idea about her home life, only that some man with a big car would collect her at the end of term. And that they embraced. *Embraced* was the word she used, not cuddled or kissed or anything like that.'

Rigby was staring at his cup of tea as if it had just landed from outer space. 'I always hoped she'd got married, had children and was happy somewhere. But she doesn't sound very nice, does she?'

'She probably had a very tough life,' Ally said diplomatically. 'It must have been hard for her, and she had to become resilient. Who knows?'

'Who knows?' Rigby repeated. 'I need to see her again. I need to see her before she's six feet under.' He looked at his wife. 'I'll have to get permission from Kandahar, of course.'

'You're supposed to be resting at home and not getting agitated,' Cathy said sternly. 'No excitement, the doctor said.'

'I don't give a monkey's what the doctor said,' Rigby snapped, draining his teacup. 'I need to see her body. I need to get some DNA. I need to see her face again, and the mark on her neck...' His voice choked, and he hastily wiped his eyes.

'As you're no longer on the case, you'd have to go through the official channels,' Ross reminded him.

'In which case I need to tell Amir about your involvement in this,' Ally said gently.

Rigby nodded slowly. 'I think the time has come to tell him,' he agreed.

SEVENTEEN

Having refused Cathy's offers of more tea and more cake, Ally and Ross got back on the road about half past three, knowing they'd need to be home by five at the latest as the dogs would have been shut in for a few hours.

'What did you make of *that*?' Ally asked as they whizzed through Drumnadrochit again.

'What? Rigby do you mean?'

'Well yes, and his change of heart about telling Amir.'

'I think you've persuaded him to make the right decision,' Ross said. 'He's obviously determined to see the body again and request a DNA test. I don't think he's going to be getting back to work in the near future, and certainly not in time to get this case sorted out. So at least by visiting his sister's body, he can get some sort of resolution.'

Ally nodded. 'I agree with you. I think I owe it to Rigby to help put his mind at rest, which he can't do himself. I need to get back to my board and think some more about my chief suspect.'

As she spoke, Ally had a further thought. If Jodi's baby had been a girl, could any of the women possibly be the daughter?

Age-wise that eliminated Penelope and Joyce, but what about the others? Was Laura the right age to be Jodi's daughter?

'You and your board! I take it that when you say chief suspect, you mean Laura?'

'Yes. I mean why else would she have signed up for this writers' course where Jodi was the main attraction? And couldn't that be the reason? To kill Jodi?'

'Or maybe to improve her writing skills?' Ross suggested.

'Unlikely,' Ally retorted. 'I think she was in constant touch with her lover, Owen Jones, told him she'd done the deed, and so it would be safe for him to appear – the so-called grieving husband! He told her where he was parked, and that's where she went every day instead of socialising with the others.'

'That makes sense I suppose,' Ross agreed. 'But what about Joyce?'

'Poor Joyce!' Ally said. 'I suppose she could have seen Laura and Owen together somehow and put it together the way we have? And I can still see Brigitte looking through Jodi's diary and guiltily putting it down when she saw me.'

'Perhaps she was just being nosy? It's the kind of thing any of us might do, and especially a writer who's always on the lookout for new stories. You could always ask her,' Ross said as they passed the sign for Fort Augustus.

'Ask her what?'

'Ask her why she was in there in the first place? Her excuse about having a look at the room or whatever seems a bit wobbly to me.'

'I suppose so,' Ally reluctantly agreed. 'She did explain that she had a pre-arranged meeting, so I can't very well come out and accuse her of murder, can I?'

'But the most important thing right now is to tell Amir about Rigby's involvement in all this, so they can hopefully get the DNA test done.'

'I will,' Ally agreed, delving into her bag and getting out her phone.

When they got home, Ross took both dogs for a walk, and he'd hardly gone when Amir arrived.

'You're going to need some strong tea, Amir,' Ally said as she led the way into the kitchen. 'Or a wee dram?'

'I'll settle for the tea, please,' Amir said, sitting down at the kitchen table and removing a file and a phone from his briefcase. 'You've something to tell me?'

'I certainly have,' Ally said. 'I've just been to see Bob Rigby. He's been keeping some information from you until now, but finally we've persuaded him to let me tell you about it.'

Amir looked up with a frown. 'Go on.'

Ally handed him a mug of strong, black tea with one sugar. 'He got a massive shock when he saw Jodi Jones's body,' she said, 'because he had reason to believe it was his long-lost sister.'

Amir, who had the mug of tea halfway to his mouth, laid it down again with a shaky hand.

'What?'

Ally then proceeded to tell him about the family resemblance and the birthmark.

'Why in God's name did he not tell me this?' Amir asked, shaking his head in disbelief.

'Because he didn't want to be taken off the case.'

'But, Ally, with his health issues, it would be very unlikely that he'd be back on this case anyway.'

'He also wants to ask you if he can see Jodi's body again before the burial,' Ally continued, 'and he would like to request a DNA test. I guess he needs to find out for sure one way or the other.'

'I'll have to arrange something with the undertaker's in

Inverness,' Amir said. He thought for a moment. 'Could the shock have brought on his heart problem, I wonder?'

'I think it's very likely,' Ally replied. 'Rigby and his family always thought she'd gone away because she was pregnant, although Rigby was only a little boy at the time. He learned most of it later, but it ties in with the magazine article about her baby.'

'Yes, but, Ally, where is this child? I've been looking into it since we last talked and there's still no sign of them,' Amir said gloomily, draining his tea. 'I must be off, but, as always, if you come across anything else of interest, please get in touch with me immediately.'

'I will,' said Ally as she accompanied him to the door.

'I don't know about you,' Ross said, when he and the dogs returned, 'but we've had a very long day and I, for one, am knackered.'

Ally reminded herself that he'd done all the driving to Inverness and back, and that it had indeed been a very long day. The lights were on in the bedrooms upstairs, so she assumed that all the women were in, and locked up the house while Ross boiled the kettle for cups of tea.

'We won't talk about this any more tonight,' he repeated sternly as she re-entered the kitchen. 'We can talk about the weather, the price of fuel, anything you like, but not another word about Rigby, Laura or anyone else! OK?'

'OK,' Ally agreed meekly. 'We might as well go to bed after this then.'

As she sank into bed and cuddled up to Ross, Ally realised how tired she herself was too, and it was only a matter of minutes before she drifted off into a deep sleep.

And it only seemed like seconds later when Ally's phone rang. And rang.

It'll be a wrong number, she thought. And then: *Nobody rings at this time of night unless... Oh no, please God, not one of the children...*

Ally groped frantically for the phone, almost dropping it on the floor in her panic. Ross groaned and sat up in bed.

It was the earl.

'Oh, Alison! I'm truly sorry to bother you at this time of night,' he said, 'but it's Magda! She thinks she's in the final stages of labour and I don't know what the hell to *do*! She says there isn't time for me to get her to Inverness as planned.'

'Have you called the doctor or anyone?' Ally asked desperately.

'Well, I tried old Doctor Hayward, who I know has been retired for years, but he must have delivered countless babies in his time. But he's not answering. I've rung the emergency services, but we're so out of the way...' He let that sink in for a moment or so, then his voice rose, 'And I don't know what to *do*!' His voice wavered. 'Could you possibly come up?'

'I'm no expert on childbirth!' Ally exclaimed, but at the same time, she slid out of bed, while looking around for her bra and digging some knickers out of her bedside drawer.

'But you've had children and you must have *some* idea—' Hamish's voice broke, and, in the background, Ally could hear Magda yelling.

'I'll be up shortly,' Ally said. She laid down the phone and saw Ross climbing out of bed as well.

'You don't need to come, Ross,' she said, pulling on a sweater and jeans. 'This is possibly a false alarm because I don't think she's due yet, but Magda's yelling and Hamish is in a hell of a state.'

'You're not going out there on your own at this time of night!' Ross said firmly as he too searched around for some clothes.

'But it's only up the road...' Ally began.

'I'm coming with you,' Ross said. 'Besides which I've delivered literally thousands of puppies, calves, foals, you name it! Delivering a baby person can't be that much different!'

EIGHTEEN

Ally had rarely seen the earl agitated. She had seldom seen Hamish Sinclair as anything other than somewhat debonair, suave and firmly in control, so the wide-eyed, tousle-haired wreck who greeted them in the Great Hall came as something of a surprise.

'They're coming, they're coming,' he exclaimed as he led them up to the large first-floor bedroom, where a writhing Magda was sweating and swearing like a trooper.

'Oh God!' she yelled when she saw Ally. 'Tell him to get some towels and hot water!' Her body racked again, and she shouted lustily.

Hamish appeared to be rooted to the spot with sheer terror. Ally took his arm, turned him towards the door and ordered him to find some clean towels and boil lots of water.

'Towels?' he asked, looking around vaguely.

Ally realised then that Hamish had probably little or no idea where anything was kept.

'Where are Mrs Fraser and Mrs Jamieson?' she asked, referring to the housekeeper and the cook, just as Magda emitted a further shriek.

'In bed, I expect,' he said. 'But I didn't think to call them because they've not had children and—'

'At least they'd know where the bloody towels are kept!' Ally exclaimed. 'And they'd get some water boiling!'

'I'll wake them,' Ross said. 'I think I know where their quarters are – at the back, on the ground floor?'

Hamish nodded mutely. He turned to Ally. 'There's two of them, you see. Babies.'

'Yes, I'm aware of that, Hamish. Let's just concentrate on one for the moment.' Ally pulled a chair up and sat down next to Magda, who was bracing herself for the next contraction.

'Will they come together?' Hamish asked anxiously, and Ally wondered how one man, well into his seventies, could be so completely ignorant.

'No, Hamish, they won't come out arm in arm, if that's what you mean. They'll come out one at a time,' Ally retorted, praying that someone would come with some towels soon because these births were looking imminent. Why hadn't she insisted that Hamish wake up the two women, because she really wanted Ross to be with her now? After all, Magda was having *twins*, for God's sake!

Ross came back into the room. 'How are things progressing?' he asked.

'I'm not too sure because I've never been down this end before!' Ally said. 'Come and have a look.'

Ross sat down and took Magda's hand. 'Don't you worry,' he said, 'you're doing fine. And I can't tell you how many little ones I've brought into this world. They might not have been baby boys, but all newborns arrive in very much the same way!'

At that moment, Mrs Fraser stumbled in, in her dressing gown and slippers, with an armful of pristine white towels. 'We got lots of water comin' on to boil,' she said, glaring at Hamish. 'Have ye never once noticed the airing cupboard?' she asked him, but any reply was drowned out by another ear-shattering screech.

Ross turned to Mrs Fraser. 'Could you possibly go back down to the kitchen and put a pair of sharp scissors into a jug of boiling water? And find some bag clips.'

'Bag clips?' she asked, looking at him as if he was mad.

'Bag clips,' he repeated. 'We'll need them for the cords.'

Hamish was now fussing over his wife, wiping her brow and murmuring words of comfort which were completely inaudible due to Magda's yelling and swearing. Ally was impressed with her considerable vocabulary of profanities.

Hamish was on the phone again. 'Still no reply from the doctor,' he said.

Ross nodded. 'Magda. It's time for you to push.'

'Push! Push, Magda!' Ally shouted. 'Come on! Give it everything you've got.'

'I'm too tired!' wailed Magda. 'I'm bloody done!'

'No, you're not! Come on! Push hard – now!' Ally grasped Magda's hand tightly.

'I can't do this any more!' Magda shouted, tears running down her cheeks, then screamed as another contraction racked her body.

'Yes, yes, you damn well can!' Ross shouted back. 'Come on, Magda – *push*! I think I can see the baby's head. Nearly there, Magda! Another push!'

'I can't!'

'Yes, you can!' Ally helped her to lean forward a little, watched by Mrs Fraser, standing agog, never having experienced anything of this nature before. Hamish was standing alongside her staring at his son slowly coming into the world, and Ally could hear Ross speaking soothing words of encouragement to Magda.

At that moment, the first heir to the earldom of Locharran for more than seventy years slid into the world with a lusty yell.

'Och, you're managing just fine,' said Ross, looking from Magda to Ally. 'Now, let's see what the other wee chap's doing in there.'

Ally had wrapped the firstborn in a towel and laid the baby on Magda's breast. She wondered if Hamish was up for cutting the umbilical cord. He was staring in awe at his tiny son, and then appeared horrified as Ross handed him the scissors. 'Come on, Hamish – it's your son!'

Hamish suddenly awoke from his stupor. He picked up the scissors and did as he was told. There was a further shout from Magda, and the second baby boy entered the world.

They both seemed perfectly healthy and extremely noisy. It was at that moment that they heard the ambulance arrive, and shortly, two paramedics came rushing into the room.

Ross, who fortunately thought about such things, had noted the time of their births as 12.31 and 12.48 a.m. and given the information to the paramedics.

Mrs Fraser was in tears, and Ally realised she was crying too. There was something about the miracle of birth that was so emotive. Hamish was fussing around Magda who, sitting up with a towel-wrapped baby in each arm, was now looking ecstatic.

Hamish had found his voice again after being rendered speechless by the whole experience.

'We must give them names!' he exclaimed. 'Ross, you helped to deliver my first son, so you must choose a name.'

Ross shrugged. 'I think you and Magda must choose, Hamish. They are the heirs, after all, so a suitable name has to be found.'

'No, Ross, and you too, Ally,' Magda said, never taking her eyes off her two babies. 'You helped me so much, and I would like you to choose a name each, please.'

'Whew! I don't know...' Ross said.

'What's the name of your late son?' Hamish asked.

Ally realised that Ross, too, suddenly appeared to be on the verge of tears. He seemed to be finding it hard to speak. 'Alan,' he whispered.

'That's a lovely idea, Ross,' Ally said. 'Alan would be a good name.'

Ross nodded wordlessly.

'That's decided then; and, Ally, what was the name of your husband? Or your son?' Hamish asked.

'Well, my husband was Ken, and my son is James,' Ally replied.

'Kenneth! That's a grand Scottish name!' said Hamish. 'Kenneth James Sinclair!'

'And I like William because it was my grandfather's name,' said Magda, 'and I would like the second one to be William Alan.'

The midwife arrived, smiling and declaring, 'Hello, I'm Katy. Looks like you've done just fine without me though.' With that, she withdrew some scales from her bag. 'Let's see what these handsome wee boys weigh.'

The babies, yelling at being exposed to the elements, were weighed. Kenneth James Sinclair weighed exactly six pounds and four ounces, and his brother, William Alan, was just one pound less. Both were pronounced healthy and to be an excellent size for twins, despite their early arrival.

Ally didn't sleep a wink. The enormity of what she'd witnessed – the birth of two healthy babies who were heirs to the earldom, after all these years! Hamish's banker cousin in London who, until now, had been the only heir, would be feeling pretty choked when he found out, and his wife even more so. Ally hadn't liked either of them when she'd met them in the past, and, more importantly, the earl didn't like them much either.

And what would Ken, her late husband, and James, her son, think about having the Honourable Kenneth James Sinclair named after them? Ally's thoughts turned to Ross, who was doing a fair amount of tossing and turning, probably thinking about Alan, the son he'd lost years ago, now remembered forever in the middle name of the Honourable William Alan Sinclair.

Katy, the midwife, had dealt with everything promptly and efficiently and promised to come back in the morning. Goodness only knew how Magda would cope overnight – or what was left of it. When Ally had last seen her, she was sitting up, her eyes shining as she fed both babies at once. Hamish, meanwhile, had seemed absolutely stunned by the whole procedure.

At five o'clock, Ally gave up on the idea of sleep and decided she might as well get up. To her surprise, Ross got up too.

'I think I dozed off a couple of times,' he said, yawning, 'but that was all.'

'I didn't even manage that,' Ally said, 'because my mind kept buzzing.'

'It was quite a night,' Ross agreed.

'A moment in history!' Ally exclaimed. 'And you were fantastic.'

'Well, I've seen a few mammals give birth in my time,' he said with a grin.

'And do you know what was really nice?' Ally asked.

'I've got a feeling you're going to tell me!' Ross was struggling into his jeans.

'It's particularly apt that these boys have been born up there, in the castle, the ancestral seat, and not in some soulless maternity clinic somewhere.'

Ross nodded. 'She was extremely lucky, Ally. I mean Magda was getting on a bit to be a first-time mother.'

'No older than I was,' Ally reminded him.

'Maybe, but you had one at a time over a couple of years! Don't forget she's delivered two good-sized, healthy boys in one go with the minimum of fuss.'

'You're right,' Ally agreed. 'She's obviously designed for this. I wonder how many more she might produce!' Ally laughed. 'All I have to produce now is breakfast!'

NINETEEN

Ally's guests at the B&B were enchanted when she told them the news later that morning.

Even Penelope was impressed. 'My God, they're big for twins!' she boomed. 'Mine were only three-and-a-half and four-and-a-half pounds, although they're thundering great chaps now!'

'And you helped to deliver the earl's babies?' Millie asked Ally.

'Ross did much more than I did,' Ally said, 'but then he's had plenty of practice! Insists that one birth is pretty much the same as another, except that humans are a lot noisier!'

'George and I have never been lucky enough to have children,' Brigitte said with a sigh.

'We've enjoyed trying though,' George confirmed, munching on a sausage.

Brigitte turned to Millie. 'I can't remember if you told us if you had children or not?'

Millie buttered some toast. 'I have a daughter,' she said but offered no further information and so the conversation turned to names.

There followed many ooohs and aaahs as Ally told them about Kenneth James and William Alan.

'So what titles do they have?' George asked. 'Earlets?'

Ally laughed. 'What a brilliant idea! No, for the moment they'll just be addressed as "the Honourable".'

Brigitte sniffed. 'The English, they have these strange titles.'

'You could get deported for saying things like that,' shouted Penelope. 'Don't forget that you're in *Scotland* now, madame!'

'Ooh, sorry... I really meant the English *language*!' Brigitte said, placing a manicured finger across her lips.

Ally escaped to the kitchen while the conversation carried on around the subject of the aristocracy and their titles, Penelope enlightening them with her superior knowledge.

If the women were enthralled with the news, Morag was rendered speechless for a matter of minutes after her arrival. Ally had never seen her struck dumb before.

'*What?*' Morag asked when she finally regained her voice. 'You and Ross were there when she was havin' the bairns?'

'We were,' Ally confirmed.

'Oh my! Just wait till I tell Murdo!' She looked hopefully at the door, but there was as yet no sign of the postman. 'Ah, now that'll be why the earl had the flag flyin' up on the castle this mornin'.'

'Yes,' Ally agreed and gave her a brief account of the night's events.

'So the earl's missus had two boys! Well, well!' She paused for a moment before adding, 'Ye couldnae make it up.' She seemed to be trying to assimilate this stupendous event before filling the kettle. 'I'm goin' to be needin' a cup of tea before I start. Two boys, eh?'

'Two big boys, considering they're twins and they were a bit early,' Ally said.

'Oh my! Our Gordon was more than ten pounds, and it near killed me,' Morag said.

Ally had heard all this before and knew it to be the prelude to a long summary of each of the births of her own brood.

'Yes,' Ally said quickly, 'I remember you telling me, Morag. Anyway, both babies are healthy, and one is going to be called Kenneth James Sinclair and the other William Alan Sinclair.'

'And they'll be the heirs?' Morag asked, pronouncing it as 'hairs'.

'They will indeed. Kenneth was the first to be born, so I suppose he'll be the heir.'

'What's that ye say?'

'He'll be the next earl. And little William will be the spare.'

Morag sat down with a mug of tea. 'Are they still in there?' she asked, nodding in the direction of the dining room.

'I think Brigitte and George have gone out somewhere,' Ally replied, 'but the other two are still in there.'

Morag looked at the door again. 'Och, I wish Murdo would hurry up cos I cannae wait to tell him!'

'Well, it's not exactly unexpected, is it? I thought everyone in the village knew she was expecting twins.'

'Aye, she was the size of a house,' said Morag before rushing to the window to see her husband's little red van pulling up outside.

As Murdo came in and laid a couple of letters on the table, he said to his wife, 'Well, ye'll have heard the news then?'

Morag scowled. 'How did ye know?' She appeared crestfallen at not being able to impart this news herself.

'Aye, when I got to the shop this mornin' Queenie knew all about it, cos Mrs Fraser was there on the doorstep when Queenie opened up the shop.'

I just bet she was, Ally thought.

'And I hear that yersel' and the vet was there before the ambulance,' Murdo added, turning to Ally.

'We were indeed,' Ally confirmed, 'but just to support Hamish really because Magda was doing fine. She seems to be designed for childbearing.'

'Two wee lads!' said Murdo. 'Fancy that! Well, I never!'

Ally could hear Penelope and Millie going upstairs, and headed into the dining room to clear up, leaving Morag and Murdo to it.

Shortly after all her guests had set off for the day, Ally was greatly surprised to receive a visit from Morwenna. She ushered her into the kitchen.

Morwenna looked around. 'Gosh, this is nice.'

'Thank you. Do have a seat. Would you like a cup of tea or coffee?'

'Tea would be lovely,' Morwenna replied. 'No sugar, just milk, please.' She sank into an armchair and began fussing a tail-wagging Flora. 'I love your dog! I hope I haven't come at an awkward time?'

'Not at all,' said Ally, curious to know what on earth had brought her here. 'Morag, my cleaner, will be down for her cup of tea shortly, but otherwise I'm not expecting anyone to call. Do you mind if I load the dishwasher?'

Morwenna shook her head. 'Of course not. The reason I'm here is because I wanted to ask if there was any chance I could move into one of your rooms for the last few days, before we all leave after the funeral on Sunday morning?'

Ally was taken by surprise. 'Aren't you happy at the Craigmonie?'

'Oh, the Craigmonie's fine, but it's just that I'm a bit lonely now that Della's gone.'

'What about Laura?'

Morwenna pulled a face. 'She insisted on having her own room, and I don't know why because she's never there. I've no idea what she does or where she goes because she's not very communicative and never invites me along. It would be nice to have some company in the evenings and at breakfast in the morning.'

Ally handed her a mug of tea. 'Well, both Millie and Penelope have occupancy of twin-bedded rooms so you could ask them if they'd be prepared to share, I suppose. They've paid individually for the rest of this week so you'd have to settle that with them.' Ally paused. 'So you've no idea where Laura goes to?'

Morwenna shook her head. 'None at all. Normally I'd just pack up, leave early and go home, but, like the others, I want to stay for the funeral.' She sipped her tea. 'I think I told you that Jodi stole my then-husband years ago?'

'Yes, you did.'

'And she soon got rid of him. He's never got over it, but I did. I left him and went on to find happiness again, but we kept in touch. Sadly, he's now in a hospice in Swansea with only a short time to live, and I called in to see him on my way up here. What he really wanted was a visit from Jodi before he died, and that's one of the reasons I came to Locharran, to try to persuade her to visit him one last time.'

Ally sat down opposite her. 'I did wonder why you had chosen to come on a course run by a woman who broke up your marriage.'

'I promised Tom I'd do everything I could. I tried writing to her but never got any reply. I thought that if I got to know her a bit on the course, and talked to her face to face, then maybe she'd agree.'

'Well, that's not going to happen now, is it?' Ally replied. 'But it was very kind-hearted of you to try.'

'No, it won't happen now, but, as you say, at least I tried,' Morwenna said. 'Anyway, Tom heard all about her death via the media, of course, and now he wants me to video the funeral, so he can say his farewells in private, he says.' She raised her eyes to heaven. 'I know that sounds a bit strange and creepy, but that's what he wants. We were happy for the years we had together, and he's the father of my only child, and he's generously supported her every inch of the way over the years. I'm still fond of the old fool and can hardly deny him this last request, so I'm here until Sunday.'

Ally had no reason to doubt her. Morwenna was a pleasant, friendly woman and incredibly loyal to her stupid, straying exhusband. She wondered briefly who Morwenna might end up sharing with for the last three nights – Penelope or Millie? If they agreed.

As she got up to leave, Ally wondered if she should have warned her about Penelope's snoring.

Ally wished fervently that she didn't have to visit the shop this particular morning, knowing full well that the place would be buzzing with the news and she was likely to be interrogated. But she did need several items, and so there was nothing else for it but to wander down there and face Queenie.

She finally got there after she'd cleared everything away and Morag had finished the cleaning, had had more tea and made more remarks such as 'My, my!' and 'Well, I never!'

As she pushed open the door of the shop, Ally was aware that the place really was buzzing, with groups of women gossiping in the aisles, and they all looked round with great interest when Ally appeared.

'We've been *hearin'* about you!' Queenie greeted her.

'Yes, I daresay you have,' Ally said.

'Ye saw them two wee lads born then,' Queenie added. 'With the *vet!*'

Ally nodded as she delved into the chiller cabinet for some bacon.

'Aye well, the vet would've seen a few births in his time!' said an elderly woman with a red coat and a red nose who Ally hadn't seen before. 'He was awful good with our Betty when she had her twins, ye know?'

Ally wondered who on earth Betty could be? This woman's daughter? 'Who's Betty?' Ally asked. 'Your daughter?'

'No, no, the *cow!*' said the woman with the red nose. 'Betty had an awful bad time calving that year, but Mr Patterson was bloody marvellous! The first one, Bella, was breech. The earl's babies weren't breech, were they?'

'No, they came out head first, just like they're supposed to,' Ally replied with a grin.

'Mrs Fraser said they were awful big,' Queenie put in.

'Big for twins,' Ally confirmed. 'And the fact they were early.'

'Mrs Fraser wiz sayin' that the earl's missus needed stitching,' Queenie added.

'Aye, well,' said Mrs Red Nose, 'she'll no likely be wantin' his lordship anywhere near her for a bit, will she?'

A tiny elderly woman, with a crocheted green beret perched jauntily on top of her golden curls, had emerged from behind the aisle of tins. 'Aye,' she agreed, 'and the earl's no goin' to be likin' that, is he? Randy old bugger!'

'He'll be off back to that Englishwoman with the funny name, up at Loch Trioch,' said Queenie, 'and you mark my words!'

'I think you're being very unkind,' Ally said. 'The earl has finally met his match, and he and his wife are very happy together.'

There was silence as Ally paid for her groceries.

An hour after Ally got home, Hamish rang.

'Magda and I were wondering if you and Ross would like to

join us for afternoon tea? And maybe a wee drop of something to wet the babies' heads?'

'Unfortunately, Ross is having to do an afternoon shift at the surgery today, but I'd love to pop in to see your wee lads, but only for a short time.' *Magda might not be exhausted, but* I *am,* Ally thought. She wondered again how Magda would cope, having refused help of any kind, and remembered her own bewilderment when Jamie was born and she'd been left on her own all day to manage as best she could. She recalled that she'd rarely got out of her nightdress before lunchtime. If then.

She didn't feel she could arrive empty-handed on such an auspicious occasion so she looked round desperately for something to take with her, and then found the bottle of champagne she had lurking in the fridge for an appropriate occasion. This was it.

As she walked up to the castle, Ally smiled as she saw the flag flying on top of the turret. Was there ever a better occasion to celebrate? When she reached the door, even Mrs Fraser was smiling, which was a miracle in itself.

'Oh, they're right bonny wee lads!' she enthused as she accompanied Ally to the Sinclair room. 'I'm never goin' to forget seein' them comin' into the world!'

On entering the room, Ally was impressed to see that Magda was not only fully made-up and dressed, but appeared composed too. She had to remember, of course, that Magda did not have to do any cleaning, shopping, cooking or any domestic chores, and doubtless Mrs Fraser would be glad to help with the babies too. She kissed both Magda and Hamish on the cheek, handed over the champagne and walked across the room to admire the two babies, sleeping soundly together in a large wicker cradle.

'How kind!' said Hamish, expertly opening the champagne and pouring some into three flutes which just happened to be on the sideboard.

'Thank you so much for last night,' Magda said. 'I'm not sure I could have kept going if it wasn't for you and Ross.'

'It was a privilege,' Ally said truthfully, accepting a glass from Hamish. 'You did so well! I think you must be designed to have babies.'

Just then, Mrs Fraser came trundling in with her trolley-load of goodies.

Magda stood up and, after glancing briefly at her sleeping sons, helped herself to a mountain of sandwiches. 'I keep feeling hungry,' she explained as she sat down again.

Hamish, apart from admiring his sons every couple of minutes, wanted to know how the murder enquiries were going, and did she think that this Kandahar fellow was up to the job.

'Most definitely,' Ally assured him, 'but he's got a lot on his plate.'

'I hope you're not in danger,' Magda said, attacking a second sandwich.

'Oh no, I'm fine,' Ally replied. 'I do realise I could have a murderer under my roof, but I don't honestly think they'd have reason to kill me.' *Yet*, Ally thought. *Perhaps they will if I appear to be asking too many questions.* She thought briefly about poor Joyce and nibbled on her smoked salmon sandwich. 'I feel we might be coming to a conclusion,' she added hopefully.

At that moment, one of the babies began to wail, and then the other one joined in. Hamish lifted one of them out of the cradle and handed him to Ally, who hastily replaced her sandwich on the table. It was several years since she'd handled a newborn, and that sense of awe and wonder came flooding back. It was also years since she'd seen babies swaddled, as these two were.

'Can I unwrap him?' she asked Magda, who was comforting his brother.

'Yes, of course.'

As Ally unwrapped the baby, having no idea which one he

was, she marvelled again at the sheer perfection of his tiny pink body, the translucent veins, the wispy hair and the damp nappy. 'He needs changing,' she said to Magda.

'After I've fed them,' Magda said firmly, unbuttoning her top in readiness.

'Time I went home,' Ally said, wrapping the baby up again and laying him down gently. She was stirred by the memories of her own two babies, all those years ago! There was just something wonderful about holding your own precious little bundle – even Carol, who'd howled her way through the first year!

And then she thought of poor Jodi. Would Jodi have tried to avoid holding her baby, knowing that she was going to have to give it up? Or would she, instinctively as a mother, be unable to resist cuddling it, knowing the heartbreak that was to come? For the first time, Ally felt incredibly sad for Jodi Jones.

TWENTY

Ally wondered if she should contact Amir Kandahar now that she had definite proof about Laura's affair with Jodi's husband.

The detective inspector had taken over what had been Rigby's temporary local police station. This was a small bungalow owned by the Craigmonie and normally let out to visitors. Amir had done precisely what Rigby had done and had a 'Temporary Police Station' notice fixed above the door, then placed a constable with a telephone on a desk just inside the doorway.

According to Callum, it was being treated more as a tourist information centre than anything else, with visitors queueing up to ask the way to all manner of remote places.

There didn't seem much point in joining the queue if Amir wasn't there, having been informed by the constable that 'he'll definitely be here tomorrow'.

As she walked home from the castle, Ally decided it was about time she had a chat with Laura on her own. Later, when she spoke to Ross on the phone, she said, 'I really need to get Laura on her own, just to sound her out, because I can usually sense when people are lying.'

'And how are you going to do that?' Ross asked.

'I have to assume that she visits Owen just as soon as they finish their evening meal at the hotel,' Ally replied, 'so I really need to be there to confront her and have some sort of conversation. I need to be sure.'

'She doesn't sound like the friendliest of characters,' Ross pointed out, 'so, for God's sake, be careful! I think I should come with you.'

'No,' Ally said firmly. 'I know you mean well, Ross, but I think I have a better chance of extracting the truth from her if I'm alone, woman to woman, and all that. And then there's Morwenna...'

'I didn't think she was a prime suspect?'

'No, she isn't,' Ally said, 'but she wants to move in up here. I'll explain when I see you.'

'Promise me one thing, Ally. Promise me you'll see this Laura at the Craigmonie, and not, repeat *not*, at Owen Jones's van? Because he's a rough character, and I'll definitely come with you if you're going there.'

'No, I promise that I'll contact her at the Craigmonie.'

'OK,' said Ross. 'Just don't wear a scarf.'

Ally arrived at the Craigmonie at about five o'clock, unaware that all of the women were having a final meeting to sum up their previous week's experiences, and now they came streaming out.

'What are *you* doing here?' Penelope boomed as the group made their way through the reception area.

'I just want to have a macord with Laura,' Ally replied, deciding it was best to be honest. 'Just something I want to ask her.'

Morwenna, who was with them, said, 'She'll be up in her room, I expect, although I know she'll go out soon. She always does and doesn't join us for dinner.'

'Good. I'll wait,' Ally said, wondering if Morwenna had already agreed to move in with one of her guests.

'We were all wondering if you'd join us here tomorrow night for dinner?' Millie asked.

'Thank you,' Ally said. 'That's most kind of you.'

'Well it'll be our last supper, in a manner of speaking!' Brigitte remarked and looked around. 'Our treat – yes?'

They all nodded enthusiastically.

Ally thanked them again. She was on her own tomorrow evening and hadn't even begun to think about what she might have for supper, and a meal at the Craigmonie did seem to be the better alternative to beans on toast. 'I'll look forward to it,' she said as they made their way towards the door.

After a few minutes, Ally decided it might be an idea to contact Laura, in her room, via the receptionist, worrying that there might be another exit where Laura could sneak out without being seen. And she had promised Ross that she wouldn't go near Owen Jones's van.

She was also beginning to feel very tired. She'd had a sleepless night, followed by a busy day, and she promised herself that she'd go early to bed.

Just as she stood up to go to the reception desk, Laura came dashing down the stairs, wearing a low-cut top, skinny jeans and a frown, with a capacious tote bag slung over one shoulder.

'Laura?'

Laura's frown deepened. 'Yes?'

'May I have a word, please?' Ally asked.

'I'm just going *out!*' Laura snapped with a further scowl.

'I realise that,' Ally said, as soothingly as she could, 'but this is important. Can I buy you a drink?'

Laura looked at her watch, gave a huge sigh and said, 'Five minutes then,' as she followed Ally towards the bar.

'What'll you have?' Ally asked, disliking this woman more and more.

'I'll have a G&T,' said Laura.

Ally ordered a gin and tonic for Laura and a glass of white wine for herself, and then they made their way towards a table for two.

'So, what's this important thing you want to talk to me about?' Laura asked, taking a generous sip of her drink.

'Your relationship with Owen Jones,' Ally replied, knowing there was little point in beating about the bush.

Laura didn't flinch. 'What's that got to do with you?'

At least she's not denying it, Ally thought, studying her and admiring her composure. 'It made me, and the police, wonder why you came on the writing retreat?'

'The police?' Laura asked. 'Why would the police be interested?'

'I think the police want to know why all of you came on the retreat, particularly those of you who have some obvious connection with Jodi Jones. It might indicate there could be a motive. I thought it only fair to warn you.'

Laura was silent for a moment. 'How come the police haven't asked *me* yet?' she asked.

'Don't worry – they will,' Ally said.

'I came here to improve my writing skills,' said Laura.

'It seems a little strange to me that you'd choose to come on a writing course organised by the wife of your lover,' Ally remarked casually.

At this, Laura leaned forward, her eyes glaring. 'That woman was a cow!' she said. 'A controlling *cow*! She left Owen years ago, but she still controlled him. He wanted a divorce, but she wasn't having that. She made a shedload of money, you know, whatever you think of her books.'

Ally nodded. 'So I believe.'

Laura seemed to be in full flow now as she took a large gulp of her gin. 'She told him she was leaving half of her money to him and the other half to the child she gave up years ago, in her will. But we damn well need that money now to keep our commune going, and when he asked if he could have it now, she wouldn't hear of it. "You'll have to kill me first," she told him.'

'And did he? Or did you?'

Laura shook her head. 'No, but I really wanted to, and that is precisely why I came,' she replied, draining her glass. 'Someone else pipped me to the post. Got there first. I swear on my life!'

'But you did intend to kill her?' Ally asked.

'I just told you that I wanted to. I'd get some poison maybe – appropriate, don't you think? – and I thought I could perhaps pop it into her dinner or something. Or I thought I might push her down the stairs perhaps, but do you know what? When it came to it, I just *couldn't do it*. I'm not at all sad that she's dead though.'

Ally had to produce what she considered to be her ace card. 'Then perhaps you can explain why you suddenly appeared at the malthouse last Sunday after everyone had got back from the castle? And it just happened to be the evening that Joyce died?'

Laura rolled her eyes. 'I'll tell you why. I came up here to Scotland without my new pack of beta blockers, which I have to take daily, and Penelope Whatsit-Whatsit just happened to have a spare foil because she takes them too. All last week I asked her to bring them down, and all last week the silly woman forgot, and so finally, in desperation, I came up to your place to get them. If you don't believe me, ask *her*. Now,' she said, standing up, 'I'm off to see Owen. But thanks for the drink.'

She turned abruptly and headed towards the door, leaving Ally speechless.

. . .

'Has Laura given you a hundred reasons why she didn't come here to kill Jodi Jones?' Ross asked as he came in shortly after Ally got back, having walked the dogs.

Ally shook her head as she towelled down a very damp Flora. 'Have these dogs been in the loch?'

'I'm afraid so,' Ross admitted ruefully, grabbing another towel for Ebony.

'Believe it or not,' Ally said, 'Laura actually admitted that she did come here to kill Jodi, although, when it came to it, she just couldn't do it.'

'So she's human after all,' Ross said.

'She said that someone else had "pipped her to the post" – her own words – and it saved her the bother.'

'A likely story!' Ross scoffed, stroking Ebony's head.

'For some strange reason, I believe her,' Ally said. For one thing, she thought, when could Laura have gone into the kitchen to get at the insulin? She and Ross had been in there for most of Sunday evening, so her entry could hardly have gone unnoticed.

'Why on earth would you believe her, Ally? *Of course* she's going to say that, isn't she? She's no fool, that one!'

Ally shrugged. 'I know logically that you're right, but I just have this feeling...'

'You and your feelings!' Ross retorted. 'You're tired, that's what it is. It's been a long day.'

'But my gut instinct is usually right,' Ally replied, crossing her fingers. Could Laura be Jodi's love child? The way she talked about the child Jodi gave up made Ally think she wasn't, especially as in the magazine article Jodi said that she had got her motherhood back, so presumably had had a relationship with her child again. 'And it was just something about her attitude, as if she didn't care one way or the other if I believed her or not. Very matter of fact.' Ally paused. 'I'll bet you a tenner it isn't her!'

'I'll remember that!' Ross said with a grin. 'Not that we're ever likely to find out because this case doesn't look like being wound up any time soon, does it? And I assume that all these women will be leaving on Sunday, after the funeral?'

'Yes, they are. Amir says that he wants it all wound up, done and dusted, by the time of the funeral on Sunday. I suppose he's hoping to have the case solved before all the likely suspects head for home.'

'He's a nice guy, Ally, but he's no Sherlock Holmes, for God's sake! I mean, the funeral's the day after tomorrow, so I truly think he's living in cloud cuckoo land!'

'He's bound to know stuff he hasn't told me,' Ally said defensively, 'and I have an idea that just might be able to help.'

'And what might that be?' Ross asked, looking sceptical.

'I thought we might have one last brainstorming session on an idea for a story, and I thought we could use the circumstances of Jodi's death as a possible scenario.'

'And how would that help?'

'I thought I'd suggest that, if we had a final writing session here, they might be more relaxed, particularly if I could dose them with some gin and tonics and see if anyone lets anything slip.'

'I think we need to drink to that,' said Ross, digging a bottle of wine out of the cupboard. 'And what about poor old Rigby?'

'Perhaps I should ring Rigby this evening,' Ally said, looking at the pine clock on the wall. 'We don't know if he's been to the mortuary yet.'

'I'll guess he has,' Ross remarked, handing her a glass of Shiraz. 'But there's only one way to find out.'

'I thought I would phone him a little later because I was wondering if he was planning to come to the funeral,' Ally said.

'That'll depend on the result of the DNA,' Ross pointed out. 'I don't suppose he'll come otherwise. But don't leave it too late to phone him because I bet that Cathy makes him go to bed early! Which we should be doing, after our sleepless night!'

Ally laughed. 'I'll phone him shortly. Incidentally, I've been invited to a "girls' night out" dinner at the Craigmonie with all of them tomorrow evening. A sort of farewell meal.'

'The last supper?' Ross raised an eyebrow. 'Just as well I've got to be at home tomorrow night. I think I told you that these Canadians who've booked the Big Barn for a couple of weeks aren't arriving until late tomorrow evening. Apparently, their flight doesn't land until four or five in the afternoon, after which they have to pick up their car and then drive all the way up here.' He paused. 'So, while you're having some boozy last supper with the girls, what's Brigitte's husband going to be doing with himself, I wonder?'

Ally shook her head. 'No idea, but I assume he's not invited. What do you fancy for dinner tonight? I have a couple of pasta dinners in the freezer.'

'Sounds good,' said Ross.

'OK, I'll heat up the oven and make a salad,' Ally said.

They'd finished eating by half past seven, and Ally decided that, if she could keep awake, it was time to phone Rigby in case he did go to bed early. She was so accustomed to referring to him as just 'Rigby' that she still found it difficult sometimes to remember to refer to him as 'Bob'.

'Hello, Ally,' he said. 'How are you?'

'I'm fine thanks, Bob,' Ally replied, 'but, more to the point, how are *you*?'

'Improving every day,' he said.

'That's great.' Ally hesitated. 'I just wondered if...'

'If I'd been to the undertaker's?' Rigby supplied.

'Yes,' Ally said.

'I have been, and it was a traumatic experience seeing her

one last time. I also got the results of the DNA test and, Ally, she *was* my sister. My sister, Joanne.'

Ally detected a little crack in his voice. 'I'm so very sorry. But at least you know now, so I suppose that's something.'

'I'm glad to have found her, even if it was too late. It's been a strange, almost life-changing experience, and now I feel the need to talk to everyone who knew her. And her child? Where are they? Have you heard anything?'

'No, I haven't heard anything about the love child,' Ally replied, 'but her estranged husband and his new lady friend are here. And perhaps Desdemona will come along too, given she was friendly with her in university.'

'Then I have a lot of talking to do on Sunday,' Rigby said. 'I am coming to the funeral.'

'Good,' Ally said, 'so long as you feel fit enough to make the journey.'

'Cathy's driving me over tomorrow evening, and Callum Dalrymple has offered us free bed and breakfast for the night once I told him the situation. Isn't that kind of him? He was very moved by the fact that Joanne was my sister and that her death had occurred in his hotel. He said it was the least he could do, and he's also laying on refreshments for after the funeral for anyone who wants to come.'

'He's a good guy is Callum,' Ally said.

'I'm not altogether au fait with these humanist funerals,' Rigby admitted. 'But I hear that it was what she wanted.'

'I believe so,' Ally said. 'The burial site is out near Brodale, and I guess it'll be a new experience for us all.'

'I'm hoping to be able to chat with everyone who knew her,' Rigby added.

Ally wondered if she should warn him that not all the comments might be particularly favourable.

'Amir Kandahar has been quite frank with me,' Rigby said, 'and I'm aware of the fact that, bestselling novelist or not, she wasn't a particularly nice person.' Ally heard him sigh. 'Perhaps if our mother's attitude had been different...? She would have had to become tough to survive, of course. Who knows? Nevertheless, I'd so like to meet my niece or nephew. Do you suppose he or she will show?'

'I've no idea,' Ally said, 'but there's no sign so far, although there's been plenty of press coverage. Anyway, I shall be dining with my guests at the Craigmonie tomorrow evening, so I may see you arriving. If not, I'll see you at the funeral.'

'I'll look forward to seeing you, Ally,' he said.

'I'm sorry I can't be with you tomorrow night,' Ross murmured as, finally, they curled up together in bed, 'even if I would have to cook my own dinner and dine alone!'

'I'm sorry too,' Ally said, although she was secretly relieved that it was a "girls only" do. 'I have a feeling that I might well discover something tomorrow.'

'Do not forget,' Ross said sternly, 'that one of these women could be a killer. A double killer at that! Perhaps I should hang around to make sure you don't get attacked or something.'

'Oh, *Ross*! I wasn't planning to interrogate them or anything – just let them chatter for a bit. Perhaps I can persuade them, once they've had some gin, to loosen up a bit. I've only got tomorrow because they all go home on Sunday.' As she spoke, Ally wondered yet again if she was barking up the wrong tree. Could the killer really have come in from outside and been fortunate enough not to encounter any of the women?

'What about Laura? Will she join you?'

'I shouldn't think so, although I shall ring and leave a message for her. And like I told you, I don't honestly think that she's the killer anyway.'

'And like I told *you*, these feelings of yours are not necessarily accurate. Anyway, you'll need someone to make some sandwiches, won't you? You won't want them drinking on an empty stomach. So I'm definitely staying until the early evening.'

Just before she fell into a deep sleep, Ally could only hope that the events about to take place over the next couple of days would not induce the killer to strike for a third time.

TWENTY-ONE

The guests appeared to be a little sad at breakfast time.

'I can't believe we'll all be going our separate ways tomorrow,' Millie said wistfully as Ally placed toast on the table. Millie had really come out of her shell these last few days and seemed much more communicative.

'Well, I damn well don't think that one of us is a killer!' Penelope hollered.

'Neither do I really. But, if someone is, then my bet's on Laura,' Millie said, just as Brigitte and George appeared.

'What's this about Laura?' Brigitte asked as she helped herself to cereal.

'Millie thinks Laura's the killer in our midst,' said Morwenna, who had moved into the malthouse last night and had chosen to share a room with Millie. Ally guessed someone else had warned her about Penelope's snoring.

'Well, she is a bit peculiar,' George agreed.

Ally cleared her throat. 'I wondered if you'd like to have a final session here for a couple of hours at lunchtime? Rain is forecast so you won't be tempted to go far, and I thought I might join you? Perhaps I can provide some drinks and sandwiches?'

'This sounds a tad girly!' said George with a grin. 'In which case I'll go to the pub!'

'Sounds a good idea,' Millie remarked.

'I'll tell you what,' Ally continued. 'I'll come up with a subject on which we can all brainstorm ideas. Perhaps you could either write a short story, or perhaps you could use some of the ideas in your next novel? How does that sound?'

'I'm up for it!' Penelope said. 'Then we can have a nap before our dinner later.'

'Yes, there'll be plenty time for a nap,' Ally assured her. 'See you all at one o'clock in the sitting room next door!'

Ally had left a message for Laura with the receptionist at the Craigmonie but didn't really expect her to appear. Which she didn't. Ally was still convinced that Laura wasn't the killer, even if she had admitted that killing Jodi had been her original intention.

When, at lunchtime, Ally entered the sitting room, followed by Ross with a large tray of newly made – by him – sandwiches, she was pleased to see her four lady guests already seated, note-books on their knees, and looking enthusiastic in spite of the rain lashing against the window.

'I'll bring coffee in later,' Ross said, giving them all a dazzling smile as he placed the sandwiches on the coffee table between them all.

'You have him well trained!' remarked Brigitte when he'd left the room.

'He's just a nice guy,' Ally agreed.

'You hang on to him then,' said Millie, 'because they're few and far between.'

'Right, I could murder a G&T!' Penelope bellowed, standing up to survey the bottles of gin, tonics, ice and lemon slices that had been placed on the side table, along with some bottles of wine. 'May we help ourselves?' Without waiting for an answer, she poured a hefty measure into a glass for herself before grabbing a handful of sandwiches.

'Yes, of course,' Ally confirmed before adding hopefully, 'I always think a little G&T goes down well at this time of day!'

'Agreed!' said Brigitte, standing up to serve herself.

Morwenna giggled. 'I don't normally drink this early in the day,' she said, 'but I'll make an exception! Or perhaps I should have wine?'

That left Millie, who was looking slightly confused. 'Maybe I'll just wait for the coffee,' she said, placing a couple of sandwiches on a plate.

'Rubbish!' Penelope insisted, the self-appointed bartender. 'I'll just pour you a *tiny* one!' With that, she poured out what could only, at the very least, be described as a double. She turned to Ally. 'I'm being very generous with your gin, Ally, but I shall replace this with a spare bottle I have upstairs.'

Four pairs of eyes suddenly swivelled in her direction.

'I always keep a spare,' Penelope continued blithely, oblivious of the attention focussed on her, 'just in case I run out. I always have a couple in the evenings you know.'

Ally resisted the temptation to laugh as Penelope sat down, raised her glass and shouted, 'Here's to the final session of the Literary Ladies! Cheers!' She downed most of her drink in one large gulp.

'*Slàinte mhath!*' Ally echoed, pouring herself a small gin. 'That's "cheers" in Gaelic, or "good health" or whatever you want it to be!'

They all raised their glasses. 'Slan-je-va!' they all repeated phonetically.

Ally waited until they'd laid down their glasses and Millie had stopped coughing at the 'small one' that Penelope had poured her.

'OK,' she said. 'As you know, I used to do research for television, and I thought I'd give you a subject we could all explore together, and perhaps you can use in a story or novel when you get home.'

Everyone nodded.

'I think it would be best perhaps if we discussed it, so we get everyone's point of view, because you won't be able to compare notes easily once you get home.'

More nodding.

'So, what are we discussing?' Brigitte asked, her French accent becoming more pronounced after a few sips of gin. She, too, had helped herself to a couple of smoked salmon sandwiches.

Ally took a deep breath. 'What I thought we might talk about is...' She hesitated for a moment, then continued, 'Would you accept the challenge if someone offered you a million pounds to do something?'

'Like what?' Brigitte looked puzzled.

'Oh, I don't know... perhaps something you'd never contemplate doing in a million years, like jumping from a plane if you're scared of heights, that sort of thing. How about you write for twenty minutes or so, and then we can talk about what you've come up with?'

They all nodded and began to write. Ally watched for a moment, wondering what her own bête noire would be. She didn't like heights either, or snakes or any reptile. She left the room to give them a few minutes and re-entered to find them all chattering.

'We're all listing much the same things, I think,' Millie said.

'OK then,' Ally said, taking a big breath. 'Would you kill someone for a million pounds?'

A buzz of conversation followed a short silence before Penelope said, 'Are you trying to find out which one of us might be the killer, Ally?'

'No,' Ally said, 'I'm *not*. I have no idea if any one of you is a killer. I'm leaving that to the police. I just want to know how you'd handle this situation. It's an *exercise*, for goodness' sake!'

Everyone was staring at the notepads on their knees.

Penelope, as usual, was ready to go. 'Well,' she said, 'if someone paid me a million pounds, I'd do whatever they asked!' She ignored the gasps. 'Keeping my horses looked after throughout the winter does *not* come cheap!' She paused to let this fact sink in. 'I'd probably find some poison or something, or crush up some pills to pop into their dinner.' With that, she helped herself to a further couple of sandwiches.

Ally couldn't quite believe what she'd heard because that was precisely what Penelope had been accused of, years ago, according to Hamish.

Almost as if she suspected what Ally was thinking, Penelope added, 'I'm quite au fait with this, you know, but I'd need a couple more gins before I tell you more.'

'Oh, do go on!' said Millie and Brigitte in unison.

'No, no,' Penelope said firmly, then added, 'Perhaps later.'

'I couldn't kill anyone,' Morwenna said quietly, 'not even for a million pounds. I could only do it to relieve someone of their misery.' She looked around at their expectant faces. 'Like a dog or cat,' she added awkwardly.

Ally knew she wasn't talking about that.

Morwenna thought for a moment. 'Maybe, like Penelope, I could spike their drink or something, but if I had to do it, I certainly couldn't do anything close up, like stabbing, because I couldn't deal with the blood, ugh! Perhaps I could shoot someone, but from a distance. Perhaps the heroine in my books could kill someone with a laser? Don't forget I write fantasy.' She sat back in her chair as if relieved to have got this off her chest.

Then Millie put up her hand a little hesitantly. 'I could never have done what that wicked person did to Jodi. Like Morwenna, I'd have to annihilate someone from a distance. Maybe cut the brakes, if they had a car, or put some explosive device in their car, and then get away as quickly as possible.' She turned to Brigitte. 'Your turn.'

'Help yourselves to top-ups!' Ally encouraged them, seeing that the contents of all the glasses, including Millie's, were fast disappearing. Could that be due to guilty consciences?

'OK,' said Brigitte, draining her glass. 'I think I could kill someone close up if I had to. *Of course* I would, if they were planning to kill me! I would try to wrestle from them whatever it was they planned to kill me with, and then kill them.'

'But,' Ally reminded them, 'you were asked if you'd kill for a million pounds, not if your life was in danger.'

There was silence for a moment as Brigitte began scribbling on her notepad.

'Could any of you strangle someone?' Millie asked. 'Like what happened to Jodi?'

There was a collective intake of breath.

Brigitte, apparently unfazed, stood up. 'Of course I would, if they were trying to strangle me!' She looked at the other three. 'But Jodi Jones was not, repeat *not*, trying to strangle me.'

'I didn't say she was,' Millie said, on the defensive. 'I'm just pointing out a method you *could* have used if she had. That's what Ally asked for, isn't it, Ally?' She turned to Ally, who was still standing by the door.

'Well, not really,' Ally replied, 'because I was really thinking about money, but it's very interesting how your ideas have developed and you've all given very intriguing answers, which hopefully you can use in your writing.'

Penelope guffawed. 'I suppose we must await Laura's thoughts on the subject!'

'You don't think *she* did it, do you?' asked Morwenna.

'Yes, I bloody well do! And if it wasn't her, then it must have been Della,' bellowed Penelope, looking around. 'I can't imagine any of us would do such things! I still think the police were extremely premature in permitting that Della woman to go, just because some bloke in the bar saw her at a distance. Bloody ridiculous!'

'He had probably had a few drinks anyway,' Brigitte added for good measure, draining her glass. 'My God, I enjoyed that! But I must not get into the habit of drinking the alcohol at lunchtime.'

'But you're *French*!' Penelope reminded her. 'I thought the French drink all day.'

'No, they do not!' Brigitte snapped. 'They drink with their food or for special occasions.'

'This *is* a special occasion,' Millie said, 'because this time tomorrow we'll all have packed up and be ready to leave.'

'After we've been to that damned funeral,' said Penelope.

Ally decided she should enlighten them about Rigby. 'We all need to act with decorum tomorrow,' she said, looking around, 'because Jodi Jones turned out to be the long-lost sister of Detective Inspector Rigby, the gentleman who had the cardiac arrest at the hotel after Jodi was discovered. Which was probably due to finding out that she *was* his sister.'

There were exclamations of horror all around.

'That poor man!' Penelope said. 'How awful! I think I'm going to need another G&T.' She looked around. 'Anyone else?'

'Just a wee one then,' agreed Millie, following her to the table and looking more animated than Ally had ever seen her before.

'Oh my goodness,' said Morwenna, 'so maybe I'll keep you company then, but only for a few minutes!'

'*Moi aussi!*' said Brigitte, plainly unaware that she'd lapsed into her native tongue.

'I should make sure you all have a couple of hours' sleep this afternoon,' Ally said, looking around and belatedly wondering about having supplied so much gin. 'What time do we leave here for dinner?'

'Seven o'clock!' said Penelope firmly, draining her glass.

Ally picked up the now empty sandwich tray and left them all to it. If their tongues were loosened a little with the gin and perhaps some wine later, the conversation could be extremely relaxed and might well provide a valuable clue.

'You're sure it was a good idea to let them loose on the gin at lunchtime?' Ross asked a little later, looking a little perplexed as he and Ebony prepared to leave at half past five.

'Oh, they'll have slept that off by now,' Ally said dismissively.

'No harm in hoping,' Ross said as he held her in his arms. 'Just behave yourselves! I'll be back first thing in the morning with a sombre suit and a black tie, and we'll set off for this muddy field at about quarter past ten.'

After he'd gone, Ally let Flora out into the garden, while she went up to her bedroom and decided what she was going to wear, finally opting for her cream silk blouse and black, tailored trousers. It wasn't cold, but it was damp, so she decided to wear her trench coat on top. She'd learned years ago, from her daughter-in-law, Liz, that she should invest in some decent pieces of clothing at her age and buy a lot less. Liz ran an expensive boutique in Edinburgh city centre, and so considered herself to be an expert on such matters, although Ally had to admit she was usually right.

Ally surveyed herself in the full-length mirror, pulling in her tummy muscles as she did so. She could certainly do with losing a pound or two, but tonight was definitely not the best time to begin.

They all planned to walk down to the Craigmonie, rain or not, to allow for the consumption of alcohol, just in case they hadn't had enough already. Except Ally, of course, who had only had one small gin and was now looking forward to her first sip of wine.

She shut Flora in the kitchen, knowing she'd be fine for a few hours, before she went out into the hallway. Her guests arrived one by one, and so Ally had time to survey their outfits.

Penelope, not one for following fashion, was in a green roll-neck cable-knit sweater and baggy grey trousers; Brigitte sported an off-the-shoulder red sweater and black leggings; Morwenna was actually wearing a dress, a blue woollen one, and Millie arrived wearing a white jumper and a vividly patterned floral skirt. George appeared briefly, gave Brigitte a quick peck on the cheek and announced to all and sundry, 'I'm off for some Italian nosh and a few beers. I might even join you for coffee later!'

'Off we go then!' bawled Penelope in her usual bossy manner, leading the way.

Despite being damp, it wasn't actually raining, so plastic macs were hastily folded up and squeezed into their bags, 'Just in case the heavens open up later,' Millie said.

On the walk down to the Craigmonie, Millie asked, 'Does *anyone* know what happens at humanist funerals?'

'I haven't a clue,' Penelope admitted, 'but it probably involves dancing or chanting or something.'

'Oh, surely not,' said Morwenna. 'Anyway, I haven't brought any funereal clothes with me, so I'll just have to wear my beige mac.'

'I shall wear this dark-blue coat,' said Brigitte, 'because I'm mainly concerned with keeping warm.'

'I shall wear a hat,' Millie announced.

'A *hat*!' the others exclaimed.

'I always wear a hat to a funeral,' Millie said, 'out of respect. It's what I was brought up to do.'

'You brought a *hat* with you?' Morwenna asked.

'No,' said Millie. 'I went to Inverness and bought one.'

'Why on earth would you do that?' Penelope asked, stopping in her tracks.

'I told you why,' Millie repeated. 'Out of respect.'

By this time they'd arrived at the hotel and the subject of what to wear was discontinued. As Ally followed them into the restaurant, she wondered if she'd been too generous with the gin earlier and that it hadn't loosened things up *too* much...

TWENTY-TWO

The round table beside the window in the Craigmonie dining room was set for six, beautifully laid out with crystal glasses and gleaming silverware. An elaborate arrangement of white roses had been placed in the centre. Ally was pleased to see that the elusive Laura had decided to join them, so perhaps the thought of a final cramped evening in Owen's camper van had lost its appeal.

The dining room was, at the moment, half full. As they seated themselves around the table, Ally found herself between Penelope and Morwenna.

'First things first!' said Penelope. 'Let's get some wine ordered!'

There was murmured agreement, and the waiter, Sam – who also happened to be Morag and Murdo's son-in-law – was duly taking a note of their wine requirements when Callum appeared.

'Welcome, ladies, and I'm sorry this will be the final evening that we'll have your company. You've been lovely guests throughout this unfortunate time, and I'd like to send out a couple of my finest wines, one red and one white, with my compliments!' He gave a little bow, grinned at Ally and then disappeared amid a chorus of thank yous.

Laura, sitting opposite Ally, was wearing a pink-and-white striped shirt and looked almost cheerful for once, probably pleased at the prospect of getting away tomorrow.

The cock-a-leekie soup, one of the starter choices, was discussed in detail and chosen by both Penelope and Morwenna, while the others dithered over what to have. They had finally decided by the time Sam returned with the wine, took their orders and moved away.

'Here's to Ally, our lovely landlady for the past couple of weeks, with thanks!' Penelope shouted, and they all lifted their glasses and took large gulps.

'George and I will be so sad to leave,' said Brigitte, 'because it is so beautiful here, but oh, the weather!' She rolled her eyes and returned to her seafood cocktail.

'But we had beautiful weather last weekend,' Morwenna pointed out. 'Remember the earl's lovely picnic?'

'The day Joyce died,' Laura reminded them.

There was silence for a moment before Penelope raised her glass again. 'Here's to Joyce, wherever she is!'

They all drank to Joyce.

Ally, tackling her smoked salmon, noticed the wine was disappearing rather fast and remembered that they'd all imbibed a fair amount on the night of the pasta supper, when they'd first arrived. Joyce had been the only one of them who didn't drink. She looked round the table, barely able to believe that any one of these women might well have disposed of both Jodi and Joyce.

'Have you been swimming again, Millie?' she asked.

Millie nodded. 'I do like that little loch. I shall miss it.'

'Isn't the water very cold?' Brigitte asked.

'Yes, but I'm into cold water swimming,' Millie said. 'It doesn't bother me.'

The others gave little shivers and continued with their starters.

'Here's to our writing success!' Millie continued, lifting her glass again. 'And here's to poor Jodi!'

There was a mixed reaction to this.

'The copier of plots,' said Brigitte, but she drank some wine anyway.

'Strange woman,' said Laura.

'What was so strange about her?' Millie asked.

Laura looked around the table. 'My partner, Owen, who's a mile or so away in his camper van, is still legally her husband.'

There were gasps all round.

'*What?*'

'Is *that* where you disappear to?'

'*Are you serious?*'

Laura nodded.

'So you knew her before you came here?' Penelope asked, pushing back her empty soup bowl.

'No,' Laura said, 'I didn't. Jodi left Owen years ago, but she wouldn't divorce him. And do you want to know why?'

The others, except for Ally, who could guess what was coming, nodded mutely.

'Because she's so bloody *controlling!*'

'Why do you say that?' Brigitte asked, her eyes wide.

Laura laid down her knife and fork. 'Owen and I run a commune in Wales. We're completely off-grid, we've paid for our couple of acres of forest, but, as you know, everything's going up in price and some of our residents are thinking of moving on. The fact is, we need money.'

'So, what's Jodi got to do with it?' Morwenna asked.

'She told Owen she'd left him money in her will,' Laura replied, 'but when Owen asked her if he could have some of it now that we're going through hard times, she didn't want to know. She said, "You'll have to kill me first."'

'So you came up here to kill her,' Penelope stated, 'to get your money?'

There was a horrified silence as everyone stared at Laura.

'Correct, actually,' confirmed Laura, nonchalantly spreading pâté on a piece of toast. 'That is exactly why I came.' She took a bite before adding, 'But when it came to it, I just couldn't bring myself to do it. Anyway, someone else got in first.'

'Rubbish!' Penelope blustered. 'Who else would have a motive like that?'

'Maybe you should ask around,' said Laura quietly.

It was Morwenna who broke the shocked silence. 'OK, we may not know if Laura's telling the truth or not, but I think we four should all give our real reasons, our motives or whatever, for coming on this trip. Let's have some honesty here.'

Ally was now on the alert, wondering if anything new might emerge now they'd had so much alcohol. *In vino veritas* and all that.

'Why don't you start, Penelope?' Morwenna asked. 'After all, you are the organiser of this group.'

Penelope sniffed loudly and took a large gulp of wine. 'The fact is I didn't care for Jodi much. In the past, I've sent manuscripts to her for editing and critiques which, I might tell you, cost me a bloody fortune because the woman certainly knew how to charge. I thought she might give me some sort of discount because we were actually in university at the same time.' Here she paused for a further intake of wine. 'I did get a couple of things published in magazines, but they didn't make me nearly enough money to cover the costs of her editing.'

'You didn't like her, but you still came on this retreat? Why?' Brigitte asked.

'I hadn't seen her in forty years and I fancied seeing her again. And this retreat wasn't much more expensive than having her do a critique, and I could have a holiday at the same time.'

'So you weren't planning to kill her then?'

'No, I wasn't.'

'In which case, why have the police been questioning you more than the rest of us?' Millie asked, narrowing her eyes.

'The police have their reasons,' Penelope snapped, draining her glass.

'Which are...?' Morwenna asked.

'Because I have a police record,' Penelope boomed, reaching for the nearest wine bottle to refill her glass.

Predictably, this caused a few gasps, and Ally wondered if she'd tell them her story. She didn't have to wait long.

'I was once accused, and arrested, for killing my husband,' Penelope informed them, her voice beginning to slur ever so slightly.

'*What?*' The others were now staring at her in disbelief.

'I was *not* found guilty,' Penelope snapped. 'I didn't kill the old fool; he killed himself, with pills.'

'Do you know why?' Millie asked, her eyes wide.

'Yes, of course I do. He had a mistress for years, of which I was well aware, but she threw him over at almost exactly the same time as I was about to leave him for *my* lover.' Penelope paused to let this sink in. 'We'd led separate lives for years, and I have to say that it saved me from a long, messy divorce.'

Sam now appeared with the main courses, which silenced everyone for the moment. Ally noticed with some amusement that the elderly couple sitting at the nearby table had been listening in avidly to the conversation. They'd been chatting when they'd all first arrived, but as the confessions were taking place and the conversation had increased in volume, Ally could see that they were listening intently and cocking their heads to hear better when someone spoke in a quieter voice.

'For some reason,' Penelope continued as she cut into her steak, 'Detective Inspector Kandahar has managed to find out about this, although it has no relevance whatsoever to this case.' She speared a piece of steak and popped it into her mouth.

Everyone was now concentrating on eating, but Ally could sense the atmosphere was becoming more and more uncomfortable. She wondered what was coming next, apart from entertaining the couple at the next table and possibly others in the dining room. Ally concentrated on her lamb curry, ensuring she didn't drop any on her expensive cream blouse.

It was Laura who broke the awkward silence at the table. 'If you've all finished sneaking looks at me,' she said as she laid down her knife and fork and dabbed her mouth daintily with the starched white napkin, 'let me just satisfy your curiosity and assure you, on my life, that I did *not* kill Jodi Jones.'

Nobody spoke for a few minutes while they finished their main courses.

Finally, Morwenna said, 'OK, what about you then, Millie? Have you any dark secrets you'd like to confess? Why did you come on this retreat?'

Millie sat back in her chair and smiled. 'I'm sorry to be so damn boring, but I honestly came here because I really admired Jodi. I liked her books, and she did a very thorough critique on one of my stories. Also, I'd read up about the Western Highlands of Scotland and how beautiful it was, and I fancied a holiday.' She paused. 'I promise you that I had no ulterior motive.' She turned to Morwenna. 'What about you, Morwenna? Why are you here?'

At this point, Sam reappeared to remove their plates and hand out dessert menus.

'I think we're going to need more wine,' Penelope bellowed at him, making him jump and causing Sam's laden tray to rattle as he headed towards the door.

Ally wasn't sure she could eat another thing but noticed that no one else's appetites appeared to have been affected by these recent confessions. As they all ordered their choice of dessert, Ally decided to opt for some ice cream, not because she really wanted it, but so that she wouldn't appear quite so conspicuous as she sat and listened.

Morwenna, now tackling a crème brûlée, happily confessed what she had already told Ally – that Jodi had had an affair with her first husband, causing more gasps. At this point, she had to reassure them that it hadn't broken her heart because their marriage was on the rocks anyway, and she'd moved on to a happier life, although she still kept in touch with her now ex-husband. 'I felt sorry for Tom,' she explained, 'because he was devastated, and I'd moved to Penzance with our daughter, met my now-husband and was happier than I'd ever been. Then Tom got in touch to tell me he was terminally ill with cancer, and wanted to see both myself and Jodi one last time.'

'So you actually went to visit him?' Brigitte asked, frowning.

'Yes, I did. I felt sorry for him. In a funny kind of way, both he and Jodi had done me a favour. I was also very interested to see her again too, after all these years, and also, of course, to try to persuade her to visit Tom.'

'Poor Tom!' exclaimed Penelope, loudly as usual. 'Well, she won't be visiting him now!'

Morwenna nodded. 'No, but he knows, of course, that she's been killed, and so he wants me to video the funeral on his behalf, and the ceremony or whatever it is they do.' She looked around. 'Do you have a ceremony if you bury someone at a natural burial site?'

Nobody seemed very sure about that, other than people might give eulogies or something. There followed much scraping of bowls and plates as everyone finished off their desserts.

'I think we need some brandies now,' Penelope announced, having demolished a huge plate of sticky toffee pudding, and looked around for approval.

Ally, glancing at all the empty wine bottles, wondered if

that was wise. She could only marvel at their alcohol capacity and wonder if they'd be in a fit state to make the ten-minute uphill walk back to The Auld Malthouse. She herself had had three glasses of wine and was well aware that she'd had enough and so politely declined the offer of a liqueur with her coffee. That, of course, did not deter Penelope, Laura, Morwenna and Brigitte from ordering cognacs, only Millie admitting that she, too, had had quite enough. Brigitte was the only one who hadn't spoken yet, and Ally hoped she might come up with something interesting, or at least something she hadn't told Ally before. Ally was trying to think of some way to get her to open up and gently prompted, 'We still haven't heard from you, Brigitte.'

Brigitte looked a little uncomfortable. 'Well, I'm interested in writing and I wanted to meet Jodi Jones...' She tailed off quietly.

'I can't think why,' Laura said, slurring slightly.

Penelope let out a loud belch and said, 'Well, there's one thing I *definitely* would like to discover.' Here she dabbed her mouth with her napkin to suppress a further belch and continued, 'What I really want to know is, *where is this so-called love child of hers?*'

There was an outburst of incredulous gasps.

'She had a *child?*' Morwenna asked.

'She *can't* have had a child!' Millie said. 'If she had, he or she would surely be here!'

'How do *you* know she had a child?' Laura asked.

'Because I was at university at the same time as she was – I'm sure I mentioned that earlier – and for the first couple of months, we shared a room in some very grotty student accommodation. One day I came in to find her sobbing uncontrollably and, after much probing on my part, out it all came. She'd got herself pregnant at sixteen, banished from the family, had her baby adopted and that particular day was the baby's first birthday.'

'How incredible!' Millie gasped.

'How sad,' said Morwenna, sniffing.

'How come you never told us all this before?' Laura demanded at the top of her voice.

Several of the other diners, as well as the elderly couple, now looked round, and Ally found herself saying, 'Keep it down, girls!'

'It was irrelevant,' Penelope said in a quieter voice. 'I promised Jo – her name was Joanne then – that I'd never tell, but I don't suppose that counts now. She told me the father was a one-night stand who she never saw again. However, after the birth, she went to live with a family who were looking for an au pair and they became very fond of her. They helped her later to get to university, and it was the father of the family who collected her at the end of term.'

'It stands to reason,' said Morwenna, 'that if the child was adopted, he or she might not know who his or her real mother was. Not everyone who's adopted wants to find out who their birth mother is.'

'That's true,' said Brigitte calmly, 'but Jodi Jones's child *did* want to know.'

'How on earth would you know that?' Morwenna asked.

'Because I happen to be married to him.'

TWENTY-THREE

Brigitte looked around calmly at the sea of astonished faces.

Ally felt as if she'd been hit with a sledgehammer. Why on earth had she never suspected?

'I will explain,' Brigitte continued, sipping her cognac. She gave a wry smile before adding, 'I can assure you that I certainly did not come here to kill Jodi! I came to try to talk sense to her.'

'Whatever do you mean?' Penelope asked, frowning.

Ally was conscious of silence in the dining room and several heads turning in their direction again.

'George was adopted by the Atkinses and had a very happy life,' Brigitte said. 'But later he was naturally curious about his birth mother and was staggered to find out that she was someone called Joanne Rigby. After much research – I won't bore you with all the details – he discovered that she was the writer, Jodi Jones, although she wasn't so successful or well known back then. And when he eventually managed to contact her, she was absolutely ecstatic to find him! No other word for it – she was *over the moon*!'

'So what was the problem?' Millie asked. 'I presume there was one?'

'The problem was that she became extremely possessive of George, obsessive even. She wouldn't leave him alone and kept appearing on his doorstep with gifts – and advice. Promised him all of her money' – here she glanced at Laura, who was staring straight ahead – 'but couldn't bear the thought of sharing him with anyone else. Between you and me, I think she'd gone a little crazy over the years because her obsession grew and, when he told her that he planned to get married, she went completely over the top!'

'You'd have thought she'd have been delighted,' Ally said.

Brigitte sighed. 'Yes, you would think so. But no, she was absolutely furious. She told George he'd never inherit a penny if he married *anyone*! And when he told her about me, she referred to me as some "French floozy" – those were her very words!'

'But he married you anyway?' Morwenna asked.

'Yes, but we never told her. We've been married for ten years now, during which time she helped him to set up his publishing company, but we didn't ever meet, Jodi and I, because she flatly refused even to see me. She liked to pretend that I didn't exist. It made George terribly sad – he became awfully depressed, really quite ill.'

Here Brigitte paused, seemingly close to tears. She picked up her cognac and took a large gulp. Then she put the glass back down and took a moment to compose herself before she continued. 'George tried to avoid her whenever possible, and as far as she was concerned, I was just his "bit of stuff", necessary only to satisfy his sexual requirements but *never* to marry. Don't forget that George was forty at the time he met me, and I was fifteen years younger.'

'Unbelievable!' Millie exclaimed.

'None of that explains why you came here,' Penelope said, slurring a little as she drained her brandy.

'I booked this course under my maiden name, otherwise she would almost certainly have known I was George's wife.' Brigitte sighed deeply. 'I asked if I could have a one-to-one chat with her on the second day, making out that I needed her advice about something. All I wanted to do was to reassure her that I loved George deeply, and that I'd never interfere with her relationship with him but only wanted her approval as his wife. That was *all*!' Brigitte then broke down in tears.

'Then you and your husband must be very relieved she is dead,' Millie said.

Brigitte shook her head as she blew her nose but said nothing.

Ally also found herself feeling quite tearful at Brigitte's plight. It explained why Brigitte had gone into Room 1 and was desperate to get hold of Jodi's diary, just after she had been killed. And it made sense now; after all, would she have killed Jodi before she'd even had a chance to speak to her? And now she came to think of it, she recalled that, when he first arrived, she had thought that George reminded her of someone, and now she realised that that someone had been Jodi. She wondered if anyone else had noticed, although obviously not.

Millie, who was sitting next to Brigitte, put an arm around her and said, 'It must be a great relief to you that Jodi is gone, but you mustn't feel guilty about feeling that way. After all these years having to keep your marriage a secret!'

Everyone else digested the news in silence, and the other diners returned to eating and drinking. Low conversation resumed, except for the elderly pair at the next table, who were now openly staring at poor Brigitte.

Penelope cleared her throat noisily. 'As far as I'm concerned,' she said, 'that leaves one obvious suspect and one only.'

'Who?' asked Morwenna anxiously.

Everyone was looking at Penelope now, the air tense.

'Laura, of course,' said Penelope.

'How *dare* you?' Laura asked, looking furious.

'Not that you were likely to inherit much from what Brigitte's told us,' Penelope continued loudly, 'but you already admitted you came here to kill her!'

'I also told you – but I don't suppose you were listening because you hardly ever do – that someone else killed her before I could do the deed. Not that I could have done it anyway.' Laura was staring hard at Penelope.

'We only have your word for that!' snapped Penelope. '*Of course* you're not going to admit to the killing! You must think we're all completely gormless!'

'You have a police record, and most probably for good reason,' Laura said, narrowing her eyes, 'so do not go accusing me, you overprivileged bitch!'

'What did you call me?' Penelope was standing up now.

Ally was beginning to panic because this was turning nasty.

'Overprivileged bitch!' Laura had now got out of her seat and was advancing slowly round the table towards Penelope, with both Millie and Brigitte trying somewhat to hold her back. Penelope was standing up, stock-still, shoulders back, fists clenched and breathing heavily.

Penelope was the first to throw a punch, which completely missed Laura and struck poor Millie, knocking her to the ground.

'Stop this at once!' Callum shouted. He'd appeared from nowhere and was now standing between Laura and Penelope, keeping them apart.

Laura, saying nothing, just turned around, picked up her bag from where she'd been sitting and marched out of the room.

Penelope was now slumped back in her chair, and Callum turned round towards the other diners.

'Please, everyone, accept my sincere apologies,' he said.

'These ladies have been through a very traumatic time, and I'm afraid their emotions have got the better of them this evening.'

There was some murmuring before everyone resumed eating, and as Ally and the others left the dining room, she heard one man call out, 'Do we have to pay extra for the cabaret? Best entertainment I've had in years!'

TWENTY-FOUR

As they streamed into the reception area, Ally turned to Millie, who was holding one hand against her eye. 'Are you OK?'

'No, it's very, very painful. I'm wondering if she's cracked the bone, and I know I'm going to have the most awful bruise,' Millie replied.

'Let me have a look,' Ally said.

Millie lowered her hand and displayed the vivid red mark and swelling around her eye.

'We need to get some ice, pronto!' Ally said, turning to Callum.

Penelope who, until now, had remained tight-lipped and furious, dissolved into noisy tears as she plonked herself down on a sofa. 'I'm so sorry, Millie,' she wailed. 'You *know* that punch was meant for Laura!'

'Yes,' Millie snapped, 'but it doesn't alter the fact that I'm going to have a black eye by the morning, a real shiner!'

Callum had reappeared with a bag of ice cubes which Ally pressed against Millie's sore eye, instructing her to keep it in position. Then she stood back and surveyed the scene: Penelope still weeping noisily; Morwenna helping Millie to keep the ice in place; Brigitte sniffing and dabbing her eyes. What an evening! How could a supposedly celebratory dinner go so very wrong? Asking for motives and confessions had *not* been a good Idea. Neither was the gin at lunchtime.

Callum turned to Ally. 'Can we get them all out of here, Ally? I think we've had sufficient drama for one evening, and they've had far too much to drink.' He stopped and sighed. 'I blame myself for starting the ball rolling by letting them have the freebie bottles, but I'd no idea it would end like this. How about I get my car out and drive you all back up to the malthouse?'

'No thanks, Callum,' Ally said, 'because I think we need fresh air. We'll walk.'

'Oh my God, look who's here!' Penelope said as George appeared from the bar.

Millie dropped the bag of ice, and Morwenna gasped.

George looked at them, obviously puzzled. 'You all going back?' he asked hesitantly. 'I meant to join you for coffee, but I got chatting to this bloke and...' He faltered, looking around at the group of women, staring at him in amazement. 'What's—?'

'I told them,' Brigitte said in little more than a whisper. 'I told them who you are.'

George frowned, looking bewildered. 'Is *that* why you're all in such a state?'

'No,' Ally informed him. 'We had a little fracas in the dining room and we're heading back to the malthouse now.'

George put his arm around Brigitte. 'Probably time we all got out of here, darling.'

'No,' said Brigitte, 'can we please stop and have a drink because I need to talk to you.'

As she spoke, the elevator door opened and out stepped Bob Rigby.

'Oh my word!' he exclaimed, looking at Ally. 'What a crowd! What's going on? We were just settling into our room upstairs and I heard some commotion going on, so thought I'd come down to investigate.'

You can't change the habits of a true detective, Ally thought with some amusement as she walked towards Rigby and gave him a hug. 'It's been quite an evening,' she said, 'and you've missed the action but' – she paused – 'you might want to meet your nephew!' She indicated George standing just behind.

'*What?* My nephew?'

'This is the son that Joanne ran away to have,' Ally informed him gently.

It was Rigby who made the first move, stepping forward and holding out his hand to George. George hesitantly shook his hand and then, after a moment, the two men embraced tightly.

'Brigitte, I think you should come with us,' Ally said, taking her by the arm. 'We need to leave George here for a little while to get to know his uncle. Come on, ladies,' she said to the others, who were standing open-mouthed in amazement, 'we need to leave George here for now! Let's head home!'

The night was cool and calm, the women wobbly. They kept having to stop every few yards.

Penelope kept repeating, 'How *dare* she call me an overprivileged bitch! How dare she!' Then she put an arm round Millie. 'I'm sorry, Millie! You *know* it was meant for that cow Laura and not for you!'

'Yes, yes,' Millie said, still holding the rapidly melting ice pack to her eye. 'I know, I know! Just don't keep going on about it.'

'Why on earth didn't George tell us that he was Jodi's son?' Morwenna stopped to ask. 'Brigitte, why couldn't you have told us?'

'George wanted to keep it secret because it might have made me a suspect in the murder,' Brigitte replied.

Ally shrugged. 'I should have guessed because there was quite a resemblance.'

Penelope hiccupped. 'I'd like to go back and punch that bitch properly,' she said, turning around and almost falling over.

Ally grabbed her by the arm. 'You'll do no such thing, Penelope! You'll go to bed and sleep this off! Breakfast will be at half past nine in the morning because of going to the funeral and' – she paused – 'you've all got to be packed and ready to leave afterwards.'

There were groans from all four.

'You can borrow my dark glasses, Millie,' Penelope said, blowing her nose and then patting Millie on the back.

'I've got dark glasses of my own,' Millie replied tersely. 'I always carry them with me.'

'I'm so sorry,' Penelope said, stopping again.

'No need to keep apologising,' Millie said.

Ally had a sudden thought. 'I expect Laura will be at the funeral tomorrow, being as she's living with the ex-husband,' she said. 'So, for goodness' sake, Penelope, do *not* make a scene!'

'Of course not,' Penelope snapped, 'but it'll take all my willpower.' She took Ally's arm and wobbled her way up the final stretch of road to the malthouse.

When they finally got into the hall, Ally stood by to ensure that they all got up the stairs safely and waited to hear the sounds of the bedroom doors closing. There would be a few sore heads in the morning, that was for sure. She wondered briefly what time George would get back.

She let an overjoyed Flora out for a run in the garden, then went back into the kitchen. She was about to switch off the kitchen lights and go up to bed when she suddenly decided it was time to adjust the board. She would never sleep unless she altered it in line with this evening's revelations. She removed the picture from the wall and stared blankly at the fluttering Post-its for a moment.

Her mobile rang. She knew it couldn't be anyone but Ross at that time of night.

'How did it go?' he asked cheerfully.

'You would not believe!' Ally replied. 'I'll tell you all in the morning. Have your guests arrived yet?'

'They should be here in the next twenty minutes or so. By the time I get them settled in it's going to be too late to come round, but I'm longing to hear all about it in the morning. I'll be with you early to help with breakfast; the last one for this lot, eh?'

'The last one,' Ally confirmed before she switched off her phone and returned to the board. She thought about her original line-up and how she'd only been able to remove Joyce and Della. She felt strongly now that Laura should be removed from the twelve o'clock spot, and yet... After all, she had no evidence to do so, just that damned gut feeling. Logically though, she knew she couldn't remove Laura altogether, but perhaps lower her down a bit, say to nine o'clock? And Brigitte was hardly likely to have murdered her husband's mother, was she? She must certainly have felt like it at times, but there was no doubting that she adored her husband and so would not have wanted to hurt him. Surely it would be safe to move her right down to six o'clock?

Ally studied the remaining three: Penelope, Millie and Morwenna. Penelope must now be at the top position at twelve, because Ally had seen the violent streak she'd displayed in attacking Laura. That left Millie and Morwenna currently at seven and five respectively, mainly because they had to go *somewhere*. But when she considered it more deeply, she realised she had no evidence against Millie, and Morwenna's story was completely plausible. But, then again, they were both there and could have done it. She moved Millie up to eight and Morwenna up to four. She then replaced the picture back on the wall.

She made herself a coffee and sat down, absently stroking Flora's head. One of these women just had to have killed Jodi Jones, and she still had no real idea who that could be. She'd see Amir at the funeral tomorrow, and perhaps he might have discovered something of relevance. She had a feeling in the pit of her stomach, something akin to dread, about tomorrow. After the state they'd got into at the dinner tonight, what on earth were they going to be like at the funeral?

At least she and Ross would be able to have a quiet evening later, with no guests!

Sighing, Ally drained her coffee, then heard George come back in and go upstairs. She checked the locks and went up to bed.

When Ally woke up at five the next morning, as she frequently did, her first thoughts were that somebody was downstairs. There was a creaking of floorboards, which could always be heard when someone entered or left the kitchen. The sound only lasted a few seconds, and Ally convinced herself that she'd imagined it before she turned over and went back to sleep.

TWENTY-FIVE

Sunday dawned with a fine drizzle and grey clouds scudding across a leaden sky. An apt day for a funeral, Ally thought, as she pulled back the curtains.

Ross arrived about eight o'clock, just as Ally had begun to set up everything for breakfast. As they worked together, Ally gave him a detailed account of the previous evening's shenanigans.

'*George?*' he kept repeating. 'George is Jodi Jones's *son?*'

'Yes, I do wonder why he didn't tell us though. But I should have realised as there's quite a strong resemblance.'

'Not having seen Jodi, apart from occasionally in the media, I can't honestly comment on that,' Ross said. Then he grinned. 'I know I shouldn't laugh, but I'd have given a lot to witness that scene last night with big, stroppy Penelope hitting out at what's her name...?'

'Laura,' Ally provided, 'and punching poor little Millie, who was only trying to hold Laura back. She's going to have a real shiner this morning!'

'I should think there's probably going to be a few sore heads this morning too,' Ross remarked. 'Do you think there'll be many takers for a full Scottish breakfast?'

Ally shrugged. 'No idea. But don't forget they'll all be heading home after the funeral so they'd be wise to have a decent breakfast.' She popped some sausages into the oven on a low heat. 'Could you halve these tomatoes for me, Ross, if you don't mind? You're so much better at slicing evenly than I am!'

Ross looked around. 'Where's that brilliant, big, sharp knife I normally use?'

'Isn't it in the drawer?' Ally asked.

'Nope.'

'Probably still in the dishwasher then. I usually leave something in there,' Ally said.

Ross slid out the dishwasher racks. 'No, not in here.'

'Oh,' Ally said, 'I expect it'll turn up eventually. Use the serrated knife. Can you keep an eye on these sausages while I check the sitting room for anything anyone's left behind before they all leave today?'

She didn't really expect to find anything, but it was best to make sure.

It was while she'd slipped her hand down the side of the sofa that she found a bunch of keys, on the fob of which were the initials C and H, twisted together. Who on earth was H.C.? Or C.H.? Ally tried to think of everyone she could remember having sat in there, including the present and past clientele, but no one seemed to tally with either variation of the initials.

Millie and Morwenna appeared downstairs together at twenty-five past nine, Millie in her dark glasses.

'How's the eye?' Ally asked as they helped themselves to cereal.

'A bit sore and quite spectacular,' Millie replied, removing her sunglasses to display the swollen area around her eye, now in varying shades of black, blue and purple.

'I was just saying to Millie that it must have taken some force to deliver a blow like that,' said Morwenna, 'so Penelope must be mighty strong.'

'And whoever strangled Jodi Jones must have been mighty strong too,' Millie said, replacing her glasses.

'Because Jodi would surely have put up a fight?' said Morwenna.

'So *we* think it has to be Penelope who killed Jodi,' Millie concluded.

Ally shook her head. 'Who knows? Maybe we'll get some clue today. Now, what would you like for breakfast?'

'We've got a long day ahead,' Millie remarked.

'I'm giving Millie a lift to the airport,' Morwenna said, 'because it's pretty much on my way. But it's going to be a *long* day. Yes, I think I'll have the full cooked breakfast.'

Millie nodded. 'Yes, for me too, please.'

'Incidentally,' Ally said, 'I found these keys down the side of the sofa. Would they belong to either of you?'

Morwenna shook her head, but Millie nodded. 'Ah,' she said, 'I wondered where I'd dropped them. Yes, they're mine.'

Ally handed her the keys, a little baffled.

Penelope appeared next, looking grey and tired. 'Good morning, both,' she said, stifling a yawn, 'I hope you feel better than I do!' She peered at Millie.

Millie pushed her glasses up. 'Take a look at that! You are not aware of your own strength. And do *not* start apologising again.'

'I am suitably chastened,' Penelope said, pulling a sad face. She turned to Ally. 'I will have the full breakfast today because there's a long drive ahead for me.'

'I guessed you probably all would,' Ally said, just as Brigitte and George entered the dining room.

'*Bonjour!*' Brigitte said cheerfully, looking around.

'I'm glad someone's feeling bright this morning,' Ally said with a smile as she made her way towards the door. She stopped in her tracks when George, standing in the middle of the room, began to speak.

'I think I owe everyone an apology,' he said, 'for not telling you who I was. But I was so afraid that it might involve Brigitte, and that you might suspect her as the killer.'

'Well, she's not out of the woods yet!' Penelope snapped.

'She told you last night why she was here,' George continued, 'which was to try to talk some sense into my strange mother.'

'You never appeared particularly sad,' Millie said, sitting down with a bowl of fruit, 'and, after all, she *was* your mother.'

George sighed as he sat down opposite her at the table. 'No, I didn't come here straight away because yes, I was sad, but also relieved.'

There was a moment's silence while everyone stared at him, digesting this.

'I was an adult before I ever knew her,' George went on, 'and, at first, I was very emotional about the whole thing.' He took a sip of fruit juice. 'Then she began to try to control every damn thing I did.'

Ally remembered what Laura had said during dinner, that Jodi was a controller.

'She'd appear every five minutes,' George said, 'telling me I should do this, I should do that. And it's not as if she was lonely because she had a lover and a good social life. But I found it very draining, particularly when she forbade me to marry. We *did* marry, of course' – here he patted Brigitte fondly on the arm as she sat down beside him – 'but I never told my mother. Jodi had set me up with my own publishing business, you see, and I was very much afraid she might withdraw her money, which would have wrecked the business. I was in her debt, and I did not want Brigitte to be mixed up in any of this. But she was insistent on coming to this retreat to try to get to know Jodi and to get her to approve our marriage.' He looked around, smiling. 'At least I've acquired an uncle out of all this! It's the most incredible coincidence, and neither myself or my new uncle Bob can scarcely believe it! In fact, when we leave here today, we're going to spend a few days with him and his wife in Inverness.'

Brigitte kissed him on the cheek. 'There will be so much to talk about, to catch up on,' she said.

It had gone quiet again, and Ally edged her way out of the room.

'I heard,' Ross said as she entered the kitchen. 'Once I knew they were all in there, I eavesdropped outside the door.' He was wearing a white shirt and dark trousers, with one of Ally's aprons tied round his middle.

'So what do you make of that then?' Ally asked.

Ross shrugged. 'It feels like he's telling the truth, but *somebody* killed that bloody woman, and I'm beginning to wonder if Kandahar has a cat's chance in hell of getting this all wrapped up today.'

Morag arrived at ten and set about loading up the dishwasher straight away.

'I'll get everythin' done and dusted before ye get back,' she said to Ally, glancing in Ross's direction, 'so ye can have a nice, quiet evenin' after they've all gone. Are ye goin' to the Craig-monie after the funeral?'

'I don't honestly know,' Ally replied, shrugging. 'We'll play it by ear and see who else plans to go.' All she could think about right now was a quiet, relaxed evening with Ross. 'The dogs are romping round the garden, Morag, so don't forget to lock them in when you leave.'

'Aye, of course.'

'And have you seen that big, sharp knife? You know the one that normally resides in the middle drawer?'

'No, I haven't, but I daresay it'll show up somewhere,' Morag replied.

Ross had removed the apron and was fitting a black tie around the collar of his white shirt. Then he donned a heavy dark-blue sweater. 'I shall have my anorak on top,' he informed Ally, 'which is suitable gear for a windswept gathering in a field. It'll be cold and wet up there.'

Ally had only ever been to Brodale once and she could certainly vouch for that fact. She'd chosen a black sweater and black jeans, and she'd wear her dark-green hooded jacket on top. She had no intention of getting any colder or wetter than was necessary.

The women were now dragging their suitcases down into the hall, to be collected when they got back from the funeral. Penelope, Millie and Morwenna were anyway, but Brigitte and George had already loaded their bags into their car so that they could get away quickly afterwards. Penelope had bossily insisted on driving Millie and Morwenna to the funeral in her car.

They were almost ready to leave when Morwenna suddenly remembered she'd left her make-up bag in the bathroom and hurried upstairs to get it.

'What's taking her so long?' Penelope asked impatiently, looking down at her watch. She went to the foot of the stairs and shouted up, 'Come on, Morwenna – we're going to be late!'

Morwenna came down the stairs holding a William Morris-patterned sponge bag in one hand and what looked like a small, black notebook in the other. 'I found this,' she said, 'when I was having a final check through the drawers.' She held it out to Millie. 'I think this is yours,' she said, giving her a hard look.

At least that's how it seemed to Ally.

Millie snatched it from her. 'Thank you,' she snapped before hastily shoving it into her bag.

'Come on then!' shouted Penelope. 'High time we were leaving!'

The burial field was situated just off the narrow road which led to an abandoned church. At the gate there was a sign which proclaimed: *WELCOME TO THE BRODALE FIELD OF PEACE AND REMEMBRANCE*, and underneath in smaller letters: *Please treat this field with respect. Take your rubbish home with you!*

There was no specified car park, so everyone just pulled in to the side on the rough ground.

Heavy, grey clouds hung over the field and the moors, but at least the wind had dropped, leaving a fine drizzle behind. Brodale was particularly bleak today, with only the old, isolated church silhouetted on the horizon.

As they arrived at the field, Ally noticed the little clusters of people standing around the gaping, rectangular hole which had been dug to receive the coffin, of which there was as yet no sign although five lots of cords had been laid out on the grass alongside. This in itself was quite unusual because, as far as Ally could remember, there were normally eight cords used to lower a coffin. There would normally be, of course, plenty of mourners to qualify for the task, whereas today could prove a little tricky.

'Good day to bury someone,' Ross murmured to Ally as they tramped towards the grave. 'Suitably dark and dank.'

They made their way across to where Amir Kandahar was standing at the foot of the grave, alongside a couple of uniformed officers.

He gave Ally one of his beautiful smiles. 'Good to see you both,' he said.

After they'd greeted each other, Ally and Ross moved up to the lower right of the hole. Ally looked around. She spotted Bob and Cathy Rigby standing near the top end of the grave on the right, chatting to Brigitte and George. They were in dark clothing and wielding umbrellas.

On the left side of the grave stood Laura and Owen, the latter fiddling with a large metal box at his feet. Opposite them, near to Ally and Ross, stood Penelope, Millie and Morwenna, all looking rather anxious. Millie was almost unrecognisable, all in black: black hat, black coat with the collar turned up and the black glasses on, of course. The only brightness came from the black-and-white patterned scarf which she'd draped around her neck.

And just arriving on her own was Desdemona, clad in a long, black skirt and top, with a purple shawl draped around her shoulders and, of all things, a bright pink umbrella. She, too, stood on the left side, next to Owen and Laura.

And behind Amir, at the foot of the grave, was a handful of press, cameras and phones at the ready, all complaining loudly about what awful weather it was for May.

Ally took the opportunity to sidle up to Amir so that she could have a quiet word with him. 'I assume you've heard all about the goings-on at the Craigmonie last night.'

'I have,' he said, not turning to look at Ally but still staring down into the grave.

'Do you know about the revelation that Brigitte's husband is Jodi Jones's natural son?'

He turned to look at her and nodded, but said nothing.

'Do you think you're going to get this case wound up today then?' Ally asked with a wry smile.

Amir shrugged. 'It's not impossible,' he replied enigmatically, but as Ally was about to ask him to explain further, the hearse drew up at the gate and everyone fell silent. Ally moved back to be beside Ross.

The funeral directors slowly brought out the wicker coffin, on top of which were two personalised wreaths, *JODI* spelled out in white roses against a background of greenery on one, and *Love of my Life* in red roses on another. That one had to be from her current lover, but *where* was he? And who had organised the JODI one? Ally wondered. Probably Rigby. Yes, obviously Rigby, Jodi's little brother from years ago. Or even George?

At this point, both George and Rigby made their way towards the gate, and each of them hoisted a corner of the coffin onto their shoulders. The main funeral director shouldered the third corner and a man, whom Ally had never seen before, took the fourth corner as they headed through the gate. The fourth pall-bearer was tall, dark-haired and dressed in black, with an impressive black cape swinging from his shoulders. Who was he? The current lover, Harry Harper? She supposed it had to be. Following behind, walking slowly, was the more junior funeral director, who didn't look more than about sixteen or seventeen.

The coffin was laid down gently alongside the grave, on top of the five cords laid out on the grass. This wasn't exactly a standard burial though, and Ally wondered who exactly would be lowering the coffin into the grave.

The tall mystery man stood alone, at the top edge, his cape blowing around him, not unlike the setting for a horror film, Ally thought.

The main undertaker, who was standing behind him and slightly to one side, cleared his throat. 'We will now play some pieces of music which had particular significance for Jodi,' he said as loudly as he could, 'and then we shall hear some eulogies before we lay her to rest.' He turned and nodded towards Owen, who bent down and pressed a button on the equipment at his feet. Immediately, Frank Sinatra was belting out 'Strangers in the Night'.

Ally liked Sinatra, but it was as unlikely a number ever to be heard in this grey, remote place, and hardly had the last note drifted into thin air than it was immediately followed by some modern jazz which, looking around at the mystified faces, Ally reckoned no one had ever heard before.

The undertaker then waved a hand at Owen, signalling 'enough' as far as the music was concerned, and turned to George.

'George Atkins, Jodi Jones's only son, will now say a few words.'

Even from several yards away, Ally could see that George looked nervous. Brigitte was gripping his arm and standing close to him.

He gave a little cough and began to speak. 'Thank you for coming here today.' He hesitated. 'It's not an easy day for me because Jodi was my birth mother, which I'm sure many of you didn't know.'

Ally noticed Desdemona stagger slightly. She'd obviously had no idea.

'The thing is,' George continued, 'I can only think of my real mum as Mary Atkins, the wonderful, loving mother who brought me up but is unfortunately no longer with us. I was twenty-one years old when I met Jodi, and we took some time to get to know each other. I discovered that she very much liked to be in control, due, I'm sure, to her strange life. She was pregnant with me at just sixteen, and then had to hand me over to someone else, which couldn't have been easy. From then on, I think she felt she needed to be in control of her own life, and the lives of all the people she met. I understand that Owen here was her first and only husband, although they've been apart for a long time, and I'm sorry that this is the way we've had to meet.'

Ally saw Owen roll his eyes at Laura, who nodded with a grin.

'She was kind, and she helped me financially to set up my business, and I know that, whatever her faults, she loved me.'

George's voice broke a little at this point, and Brigitte squeezed his arm. 'She was a very talented lady and, as you know, became a bestselling author. I'm proud to have been her son, and I'm delighted' – he turned to Rigby – 'to have met her wee brother, Detective Inspector Bob Rigby here, who is my new – and only – uncle! May Jodi rest in peace.' George stood back and wiped his eyes.

A few people clapped a little hesitantly, not knowing if they should be doing so or not.

The undertaker signalled to Owen again, who, with some grunting and then some squeaks from the machine, finally produced Ella Fitzgerald singing the mournful 'Ev'ry Time We Say Goodbye'.

Ally studied the little groups. Rigby was looking impassively straight ahead; Cathy beside him was staring at the open grave. Desdemona, still alone as always, had her head bowed, inscrutable. Penelope and Morwenna were sharing a black umbrella, standing back a little and whispering. Morwenna had her phone out, filming this ritual for her ex-husband, one of Jodi's ex-lovers. Millie, slightly apart from the other two, and unrecognisable in her mourning outfit, looked to be gazing at something or someone at the top end of the grave, although it was difficult to tell from behind her dark glasses.

Owen was taking his disc jockey duties very seriously and was bent down, tinkering with a row of knobs, which kept altering the sound and volume at irregular intervals, the sudden bursts of volume causing everyone to jump.

'Do you know who that man in the cape is?' Ross murmured.

'That has to be Harry Harper,' she replied in a whisper. 'The lover and her agent.'

For a moment, she wondered if he might be involved, but a man like that – and he was quite distinctive – could hardly have nipped into the ladies' room at the Craigmonie, strangled Jodi and then nipped out again unnoticed. Ally sighed. The killer *must* be here today.

She looked at Laura, standing shivering in a thin coat just behind Owen and his machine. She still couldn't believe that any of her remaining four guests could have had any hand in this. Again, she wondered if perhaps she'd been wrong; perhaps someone *had* crept into the ladies' cloakroom that fateful afternoon and got out again unnoticed?

If Amir knew something, then he certainly wasn't telling. But it was interesting that he had two uniformed officers with him.

Were they expecting trouble?

TWENTY-SIX

Rigby appeared confident as he began to speak. After all, he must be accustomed to addressing the police and the public, Ally thought, but this was different, of course. This was personal.

'Jodi, who was really Joanne Rigby, was my big sister,' he began. 'I can only just remember *her*, but I can clearly recall the birthmark on her neck, and fifty years later, I saw it again when I investigated her murder at the Craigmonie Hotel in Locharran two weeks ago. The shock took its toll' – here he patted his heart – 'but at least the DNA proved that I was right. It was indeed my sister, Joanne.' Rigby paused and looked around. 'What can I say? Nobody tells a five-year-old that his big sister has got herself pregnant and has been banished! But that's how it was back then, a terrible disgrace, and shame on everyone concerned. Poor, poor Joanne!

'Fortunately, times have changed, and if Joanne's death produced one good thing, it's been meeting that baby she had to give up.' He smiled across at George. 'I now have a nephew and am looking forward to getting to know both him and his lovely wife.' He took a deep breath. 'Unfortunately, it appears inevitable that someone here, right here at this graveside, must have murdered my sister, and I can only hope that Detective Inspector Kandahar, who's taken over from me, will be able to arrest that person before long.'

Ally heard some gasps and saw Amir nodding.

'Jodi may not have been loved by everyone,' Rigby continued, 'because I think her life must have been blighted at times with her need for self-preservation and control. Let's face it, she had to make her own way in the world from the age of sixteen and, all things considered, she did well. Let me wind up by saying that I am truly proud to be the brother of such a strong and talented woman. Thank you.'

The undertaker nodded towards Owen again, which resulted in Pavarotti belting out 'Nessun Dorma' at full volume, until Owen, with further twiddling of buttons, managed to lower the sound to a less ear-splitting level. There was certainly no chance of anyone resting in peace around here, Ally reckoned.

'Eclectic mix,' murmured Ross.

'Yes and, apart from that weird jazz, all good stuff,' Ally said.

'We will now lower the coffin into the grave,' said the main undertaker. 'You may have noticed that there are fewer cords than normal. This is because we were unsure how many mourners would be here and also because a wicker coffin is very light indeed.' He looked around for a moment. 'Mr Harper, who is the chief mourner, and myself will take the first cord, and we've agreed with Mr and Mrs Rigby that they will take the second one, and perhaps' – here he nodded to George – 'you and your wife might like to take the third?'

George nodded, and he and Brigitte, who did not look very happy at the prospect, moved towards the coffin.

At this point, Desdemona looked up and called out, 'I'm Desdemona Morton and I've known Jodi since university days, and I'd be honoured to take a cord.'

'Thank you, Miss Morton, so perhaps you'd like to take the fourth cord with my fellow funeral director?' As they moved forward, he looked round again, this time directing his gaze at Owen. 'I understand you were her husband?'

Owen sniffed loudly. 'Yeah,' he said in what could only be described as a resigned voice.

The undertaker looked a little bewildered by Owen's tone and was momentarily at a loss for words.

It was Harry Harper who came to the rescue. 'Jodi left her husband years ago,' he said, 'but never got round to getting a divorce.' He regarded Owen with some distaste.

'*Her* choice!' snapped Owen, glaring back at Harper.

'Yes, well,' the undertaker said hastily, 'whatever the circumstances, would you and your, er, partner like to take the fifth cord perhaps?'

Laura's face was a picture. She plainly had no wish to participate in this strange and rather uncomfortable little cere-mony, until Owen took her arm and rather roughly pulled her along with him towards the fifth cord.

The cords were picked up somewhat jerkily, and Ally had visions of the coffin slipping off, but after a minute or two they got it straightened, and, slowly and gently, they all lowered the wicker coffin into the grave.

Ally felt a great sadness. The woman might not have been very popular but she didn't deserve to die in the way she had. No one did. She was only relieved that neither she nor Ross had been asked to take part. She could only imagine how Brigitte and Laura must be feeling; Laura in particular, having to help to lower the coffin of the woman she'd come here to kill!

Everyone stood silently for a moment, and Ally noticed Millie had moved up a little towards the top of the grave as if to get a better view of the coffin, now deep in the earth. Perhaps she was videoing the ceremony as well as Morwenna, although Ally couldn't see a phone in Millie's hand.

The sky had darkened further, looking almost bruised, which made Ally think of poor Millie's black eye, now hidden by the ridiculously inappropriate sunglasses, which looked so out of place in this lowering, drizzly, windy day. Along with Millie, everyone was gazing down at the coffin and moving, very slowly, towards the top of the grave.

The chief undertaker cleared his throat again and said, 'We will now play the final song which Miss Jones had requested. And then Mr Harry Harper will give a closing eulogy.' He signalled to Owen, who'd gone back to his music machine again.

This time it was another of Sinatra's signature songs, the very appropriate 'My Way'. Both Rigby and George were dabbing their eyes, while Harry Harper stood, motionless and emotionless, at the top of the grave, looking down at the coffin. Was he in some sort of trance? Or drugged even?

Ally was a little concerned about Millie, who appeared to be behaving oddly. She was edging ever closer towards the top of the grave and clutching her coat tightly around her, as if she was terribly cold. Ally wondered if she was having some delayed reaction from last night's injury. Perhaps she didn't feel too well. Ally wondered if she should go over to see if she was all right, but as the Harper fellow was about to begin speaking, she decided against it.

And now it was the turn of Harry Harper to address the gathering. He looked around a little haughtily at everyone with the air of a man who was perfectly accustomed to public speaking.

'The day Jodi was killed, part of me died too,' he said sadly. 'She was my *everything*!' He paused before repeating, 'Everything!' and letting this fact sink in. The only sound was some coughing and shuffling of feet from the bystanders. 'She was the only woman who has ever brought me true happiness, and I don't honestly know how I'm going to live without her. I know how thrilled she was to meet George, her son, and I can understand why she became so possessive, as if trying to make up for lost time.'

He then turned slightly in Rigby's direction. 'As for her little brother,' he continued, 'the coincidence is beyond belief, incredible, and very moving. It could have been a scene in one of her wonderful books. If only she could have met him again, after all those years, while she was alive! It's strange that Jodi should have chosen to come up here to Scotland, just a few miles from where her brother was working. Surely it was the work of fate, but I can only imagine the horror that Bob Rigby experienced when he discovered who the murder victim was.' He coughed. 'She was a brilliant woman, a brilliant writer and, above all, a survivor – until, that is, some evil person brought her life to such a tragic end.'

At this point, his cape billowed out, somewhat dramatically, as if on cue.

'There is one person standing here today who killed my lovely Jodi – and also murdered some innocent woman who must have worked out who the killer really was. And I say "she" because, without doubt, the killer is a woman, and' – here he looked round at everyone – 'if you've got one ounce of decency in your body, you should make yourself known.'

Ally wondered if Amir had prompted him to say that in order to provoke a response.

She then became aware, with growing unease that Millie had now reached the top of the grave and was standing just behind Harper's billowing cape. Looking at the little mousy woman, Ally realised she really knew so little about Millie Day, she couldn't even remember her full name. What was it? Millicent? Amelia?

Suddenly, she recalled the evening when they'd first

arrived. *Millie Day*, she'd said when Joyce had introduced her. *Short for Camilla...* Camilla! A recent memory sparked in Ally's brain: the key fob in the sitting room with the initials C.H. If they were Millie's, what could the H stand for? Of course, of course – Harper!

It was catching sight of her kitchen knife that froze Ally to the spot. *The knife!*

Millie was holding it high in the air, above Harper's shoulder.

'Oh my God!' Ally took to her heels. She hadn't run so fast in years, but she knew she had to reach Millie before she did what she'd plainly planned to do.

Completely unaware of what was happening behind him, Harry Harper carried on speaking. 'Finally,' he continued, 'I—'

'Finally!' Millie screeched. 'Finally, I got her, and now it's *your* bloody turn!'

Ally, frantically shouting, 'Stop! Stop!' reached Millie a split second before she plunged the knife into Harper's back, only the handle still visible above his shoulder. He crashed directly into the grave, falling on top of the coffin with a sickening thud and the crack of breaking wicker withies. In the meantime, Ally and Millie were wrestling on the ground, Millie shouting, 'I have to KILL him!' as she struggled to get free.

Ally, struggling to her feet, could hear Ross's voice shouting, 'Bloody hell!' as he and the two uniformed police officers raced towards Millie, who scrambled to her feet and was now standing defiantly, smiling, looking down into the grave. Everyone else seemed mesmerised and paralysed with horror for a split second before they could move.

'That Jodi bitch,' Millie ranted as the two police officers began to drag her away. 'She stole my husband and I've waited *years* to get her! *And him!* I hope he dies right there, on top of her! *Bastard!*'

She lashed out against the two officers, her fist flying as she tried to beat both of them at once, and the Inverness hat took off in the breeze. As the officers grappled with her to retain control, her sunglasses fell from her face into the grave, her black and blue eye contrasting with her vivid red cheeks. Her expression was one of absolute hatred as she struggled and kicked all the way to the police car, screaming obscenities and abuse.

'Oh, Ally!' Ross steadied Ally as she leaned against him. 'Oh God, are you OK? Has she stabbed you?'

Ally shook her head. 'No, Harry Harper got the full thrust of it. I'll be OK in a moment – just let me get my breath back...'

Amir had appeared now. 'What made you move like that, Ally? I reckon you've saved Harper's life by tackling her when you did.'

Ally gave a bleak smile. 'I put two and two together in what seemed like a split second, reckoning that she just *had* to be Harry Harper's abandoned wife.'

'What made you realise that?' Amir asked gently.

Ally told him about the key ring. 'I couldn't work out why it would be Millie's with the initials C.H. or H.C. on the fob, until I saw her approaching Harper, and then I remembered her full name was Camilla, and it all began to make sense...'

Amir nodded, then sped off to join George and Rigby, who were about to climb down into the grave to retrieve Harry Harper.

'Ross!' Ally said. 'You must go to help because Rigby's just not well enough to do this.'

Ross stepped forward and put a restraining hand on Rigby's arm. 'You step back,' he said. 'I'll help.'

They lifted Harper out of the grave and laid him, face down, on the ground, the mourners hastily standing back to make room.

'Nobody tries to remove that knife!' warned Amir, amidst the general chaos. 'You could cause more harm than good, and the ambulance is on the way.'

Morwenna and Penelope moved to stand beside Ally.

'This is beyond being awful!' Morwenna said, staring at Harper's body. 'I cannot believe what's just happened...'

'He's not dead,' Ross said, 'but I'm damn sure that *was* her intention, if Ally hadn't been so quick off the mark.'

Amir was kneeling beside Harry Harper's prostrate body, making call after call on his phone. When he finally replaced the phone in his pocket, he said, 'We expected trouble today, and we certainly got it.'

Morwenna had been physically sick, and was now shaking and in tears. 'I'd have been next on her list,' she sobbed, 'because I found her passport lying on the floor while we were getting ready to leave for the funeral today and her name was Camilla Harper, not Millie Day. Day was her maiden name.' She blew her nose. 'When I gave it back to her, she snatched the passport back but didn't explain.'

Ally put a comforting arm around her. 'I think Joyce probably found it too when they were sharing a room and put two and two together...'

'Millie never spoke about her life if she could avoid doing so,' said Penelope. 'We knew she was divorced, but she was very tight-lipped about anything to do with her earlier years.'

Laura had come to join them, leaving Owen to pack up his machine. 'I had no idea,' she said, blowing her nose.

'None of us did,' Penelope said, quietly for once.

Ally was finding it incredible to believe that two such different women had come on this retreat for the sole purpose of killing Jodi Jones, and another had come to try to reason with her. What a strange, mixed-up woman Jodi must have been!

And Millie! Mousy little Millie, who liked cold water swimming! Who would have believed it? She was the woman Harry Harper had abandoned so long ago, leaving her and their three-month-old baby. How she must have hated him and nursed that hatred year after year, planning how to get her revenge. Well, she certainly managed that, Ally thought, and how.

And then she heard what was now becoming an all too familiar sound. Ally looked up at the sky and saw the helicopter as a dot in the distance, and then becoming larger and larger as it neared this remote place. It had only been two weeks since they'd last seen it.

TWENTY-SEVEN

Feeling increasingly shaken by what had just taken place, Ally was glad of Ross's supporting arm around her. He, too, looked a little shell-shocked, but neither of them was as badly affected as poor Morwenna, and even Penelope's stiff upper lip appeared to be a tad wobbly. Ally realised that neither of her remaining guests were in any fit state to drive south that afternoon, particularly Morwenna. If Morwenna planned to go all the way to Penzance in one go, it would certainly take her a good twelve hours because Penzance was as far away from Locharran as it was possible to get without falling into the English Channel.

'You are both staying another night,' Ally instructed them firmly, 'and if you feel strong enough, you can set off tomorrow.'

Neither of them argued, just thanked her profusely.

'I shared that room with her!' Morwenna kept repeating, still in shock and disbelief. 'And she had killed *two women!*'

'Well, just be grateful you weren't the third!' Penelope snapped, plainly considering this remark to be of some comfort – which, of course, it wasn't – and caused Morwenna to start wailing again.

'And they've taken my *phone*!' Morwenna added, blowing her nose.

Filming the funeral for her ex-husband, she was the only person to have captured the incident, and Amir had wanted a copy for the records, promising her that he'd return it later in the day.

Ally was beginning to wonder just how much Morwenna's ex-husband – whose desire to see Jodi again was the reason she was here in the first place – was really going to enjoy watching this horrendous video from his hospital bed.

The four Rigbys – weren't George and Brigitte now really Rigbys too? – approached. Brigitte gave Ally a big hug first. 'Thank you so much, Ally, for everything! I still can't get my head round what's just happened. *Au revoir*!' Her eyes were full of tears.

George gave her a bear hug too and added, 'Thank you for your help in all this, Ally. I now know who my real parents were, even my father, who was just a lad in her class in school. Sadly he died in a motorbike accident a couple of years later. I'm not going to try to contact any of that family. No point now. But we'll be coming up here more often now to see my *uncle*! And we'd love to see you again.'

Even Rigby himself was in hugging mood. 'Thank you, Ally,' he said. 'Thank you for everything, and particularly for telling Kandahar about my relationship to Jodi. It was the wisest decision, and now I can have some closure on my sister Joanne's tragic death.'

As they were making their way towards their car, Desdemona joined them.

'At least,' she said sadly, 'poor Jodi has ended up in this peaceful spot where I can come from time to time with some flowers.'

'It's certainly peaceful now,' Ally agreed, looking around at the damp, windswept moor.

'So that murdering guest of yours turned out to be Harper's ex-wife?' Desdemona asked as they walked towards where their vehicles were parked.

'Yes, but we were unaware of that because she registered everywhere in her maiden name,' Ally said, 'and she certainly gave no clue. Didn't talk about her personal life at all.'

Desdemona frowned. 'Did I tell you that Jodi came to see me on the day she arrived in Locharran?'

'No, you didn't,' Ally said, not entirely surprised. Desdemona wasn't one to share her secrets if she didn't have to.

'She stayed for about an hour and we had quite a chat. According to what Jodi told me, Harper left his wife about twenty-five years ago. Wouldn't you think she'd have got over it by now?'

'They never divorced?' Ross asked as he unlocked his car.

'No,' Desdemona replied, 'she refused to divorce him. Not that Jodi was bothered because she wasn't divorced either.'

'So, the only person really affected by this was Millie,' Ally said. 'But Harper isn't dead, thankfully. Millie came up here purely to get rid of both him and Jodi, but had to kill Joyce too, most likely because poor Joyce found her passport or some item with her married name on it.' *And Morwenna might well have been next*, she thought.

'I'm going to see Hamish and meet his boys now,' Desdemona said as she opened the door of her old Land Rover and, after folding up the pink umbrella, climbed into the driving seat. 'I only hope that woman swings for what she's done!'

With that, Desdemona did a three-point turn, scattering mud in every direction, and was gone.

Back at the malthouse, the cases were dragged upstairs again, with only Millie's standing in isolation near to the door until Amir appeared to pick it up later, as promised. Ross had taken over and ushered them all into the sitting room to recover, offering tea, coffee, wine, whisky or whatever they fancied. Everyone wanted tea, except for Penelope of course, who wanted 'coffee with a good shot of brandy in it'.

'I wish now I'd knocked her right out!' Penelope said, taking a large gulp of her coffee. 'If only I'd known...'

'If only *any* of us had known,' Ally remarked.

'Yes, but I could perhaps have saved that Harper fellow too,' Penelope continued. 'If only I'd hit her harder.'

'Then she might never have been caught,' Morwenna said.

'I think Detective Inspector Kandahar had his suspicions,' Ally said. 'He must have known, of course, that Millie's real name was Harper. It just seems so sad that a third person had to suffer. At least she didn't kill him.'

'*Yet*,' said Penelope ominously. 'There's no guarantee he'll survive.'

'We'll have a takeaway Italian tonight from Concetti's,' Ross interrupted. 'Cannelloni OK?'

'Yes, fine,' Penelope confirmed.

At that moment, the front doorbell rang, and there was Amir. He'd come to collect Millie's suitcase, to return Morwenna's phone, and to tell them that Harry Harper was now in hospital and expected to make a full recovery.

'He had no idea that Millie was there,' Amir said, 'so cleverly was she disguised. And now Millie herself is already in a police cell and is unlikely to ever be free again. She's confessed to us that yes, she did kill Jodi, but that hadn't been her intention, but she did plan to harm her physically or confront her in some way. Then she and Jodi were in the bathroom at exactly the same time that afternoon, resulting in an altercation, during which Jodi sneered at her, causing Millie to go completely haywire and strangle her. Not premeditated perhaps, but murder whichever way you look at it.' He studied Ally for a moment. 'I must congratulate you on your quick thinking and action, which saved Harper's life. More than ever now, I look forward to working with you in the future.'

After the women returned upstairs, the doorbell rang once more, and there was the earl, bearing a bottle of his finest malt whisky.

'I've just heard the ghastly news,' he said. 'Desdemona called in on her way back from Brodale.'

'Yes, she told me she would,' Ally replied.

'Well, I thought this might provide some comfort.' He deposited the bottle on the kitchen table.

'Thank you so much, Hamish,' Ally said. 'This is more than generous of you.'

'Life has not exactly been dull for you, has it, since you came to live in this neck of the woods?' Hamish said to Ally with a rueful grin. 'But let's hope there are no further incidents like this.'

'Why don't you and Magda come down and join us for a Concetti takeaway tonight?' Ross asked.

Hamish rolled his eyes, smiling. 'I'm afraid Magda's too busy. She's walking around, organising the kitchen, with two baby slings attached, and helping to make some concoction for tonight's supper. But why don't you both come up and lunch with *us* tomorrow? Twelve noon, for lunch at one, *what-ho?*'

'Thank you, Hamish, that would be lovely.' She looked at Ross, who nodded. 'How are the babies?'

'Oh, incredible. Magda carries them around in those sling things, one on each side.' He sighed. 'Life has changed, rather – but it's wonderful, of course.'

The cannelloni was delicious, and Penelope remarked about how similar – and yet so different – this evening was to when they'd first arrived, two weeks previously, and had eaten pasta in the malthouse kitchen. 'You and I,' she said to Ally, 'are the only two from that dinner who are still here. Poor Joyce has gone, bloody Millie is off to jail, Jodi's six feet under, Brigitte's in Inverness and Morwenna was still at the Craigmonie that first night.' She turned to Ross. 'And *you* weren't here either!'

They all drank wine, they all relaxed and they all went to bed early, either to sleep soundly – Penelope and most likely Ross too – or to toss and turn and relive the day's events – probably Morwenna and very likely Ally. When it came to it though, Ally did sleep deeply, due in no small part to exhaustion – and relief that this incident was finally over.

Breakfast was a subdued affair, without much conversation. Both women wanted an early breakfast at eight so that they could get on the road. Morwenna was going to see her ex in Wales and drive back to Penzance the following day. She had a lot to tell him, and Penelope had a lot to tell her neighbours, her sons and the local paper. 'They frequently ask me for some input,' she said airily. 'And, boy, haven't I got some input *this* month!'

There was more hugging and more tears as they both finally headed towards their cars, Ross gallantly carrying the suitcases and helping stow them away. There followed much waving and tooting as Penelope and Morwenna drove their cars down towards the village, and eventually to the road south.

Before they went back inside, Ally looked around at the stunning view. The sky was clear today, and she could see right down beyond the river and the grey stone buildings in the village. She could even see lambs frolicking in the field on the far side. She realised, again, just how much she really loved it here.

Looking up at the heather-clad hill leading to the castle, she said, 'Well, now we have lunch with Hamish and Magda to look forward to.'

'And then,' said Ross, 'a lovely, quiet evening.'

'Oh yes,' Ally agreed, 'a lovely, quiet evening. Thank goodness the events of the past fortnight are over, and yet I have a feeling it isn't entirely over.'

'What do you mean?' Ross asked.

'Well, I think I can almost guarantee that at least one of the literary ladies will be writing the entire episode into a book.' She smiled.

'Bound to be a bestseller then!' said Ross. He looked at her anxiously. 'After all this, I hope you don't have any regrets about coming to live in Locharran?'

'None at all,' Ally assured him, taking his hand. 'None at all.'

A LETTER FROM DEE

Dear Reader,

Ally McKinley's been sleuthing again! She's become quite good at this, having gained experience in the two earlier novels, and she's not done yet – there's more to come! If you'd like to read these earlier Ally McKinleys, my women's fiction novels or the Kate Palmer series of crime novels, then please do sign up to the link below. Your email address will never be shared, and you can unsubscribe at any time.

www.bookouture.com/dee-macdonald

I'm always grateful for reviews and to know what readers think, so you can get in touch with me via social media too.

Most importantly, thank you so much for reading my book, and I hope I kept you guessing until the end!

Best wishes,

Dee

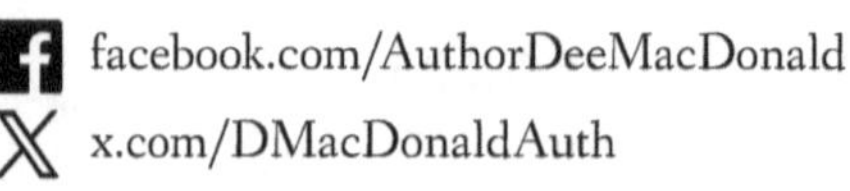

ACKNOWLEDGEMENTS

Huge thanks, as always, to Lizzie Brien, my lovely editor at Bookouture, for her brilliant suggestions and edits, and for knocking my ramblings into shape. And for being so lovely and helpful.

Thanks also to Natasha Harding at Bookouture and to my agent, Amanda Preston, at LBA. Without these ladies' faith in me, I would not be a writer.

Which leads me, as always, to my friend and mentor, Rosemary Brown, who helps with so much of the plotting and planning that goes into these books. She's the best 'writing buddy' I could possibly have!

Thanks to my husband, son and grandsons, for their never-ending support and help in sorting out my technical problems because I am far from being computer savvy.

And, not least, thank you to the huge team at Bookouture who help to produce the books, including Alba Proko, Melissa Tran, Peta Nightingale, Mandy Kullar, Nadia Michael, Sarah Hardy, Stephanie Straub, Occy Carr, Melanie Price, Jane Eastgate, Laura Kincaid and Lisa Brewster.

They are such a lovely, helpful group, And I certainly mustn't forget Kim Nash and Noelle Holten for the amazing promotional work they do. If I've omitted to mention anyone, I assure you it was not intentional and I sincerely apologise.

Finally, thanks to you, dear reader! Thank you for buying my books, for the reviews and for all the lovely messages I receive.

PUBLISHING TEAM

Turning a manuscript into a book requires the efforts of many people. The publishing team at Bookouture would like to acknowledge everyone who contributed to this publication.

Audio
Alba Proko
Melissa Tran
Sinead O'Connor

Commercial
Lauren Morrissette
Hannah Richmond
Imogen Allport

Cover design
The Brewster Project

Data and analysis
Mark Alder
Mohamed Bussuri

Editorial
Lizzie Brien

Copyeditor
Jane Eastgate

Proofreader
Laura Kincaid

Marketing
Alex Crow
Melanie Price
Occy Carr
Cíara Rosney
Martyna Młynarska

Operations and distribution
Marina Valles
Stephanie Straub
Joe Morris

Production
Hannah Snetsinger
Mandy Kullar
Ria Clare
Nadia Michael

Publicity
Kim Nash
Noelle Holten
Jess Readett
Sarah Hardy

Rights and contracts
Peta Nightingale
Richard King
Saidah Graham